PRAISE FOR *RE*

CW01455261

"Anton Solomonik's stories ar[e] and outrageously funny. As *absurdum* of the human cond their given human bodies, lik[e] they unceremoniously toss every stripe of piety, conformism, and posturing straight into the acid bath — they reverberate with a brilliant and steadfast, backhanded humanism. That is to say, *Realistic Fiction* is a grand and electrifying read."

— Paul Harding, Pulitzer Prize-winning author of *Tinkers*

"What does it mean to be understood? My heart overflows at this long-awaited story collection, which blends Sonic the Hedgehog aesthetics with the exacting interior investigations of a trans Thomas Mann, and which answers that question through unforgettable narrators who passionately strive to become less than they are, and who fail."

— Jeanne Thornton, Lambda Award-winning author of *Summer Fun*

"If you like your prose freaky, your filth ambivalent, your millennial transes confused, and your gloomy irony served with a soupçon of glamorous ideological danger, do I have the book for you. Anton Solomonik's *Realistic Fiction* is irresistible. I'm a fan!"

— Andrea Lawlor, Whiting Award-winning author of *Paul Takes the Form of a Mortal Girl*

"There is *nobody* doing it like Anton. I cannot wait to hear what people make of this collection of freaks (deeply complimentary)."

— Tuck Woodstock, host of Gender Reveal

ABOUT LITTLEPUSS PRESS

LittlePuss Press is an independent feminist press run by trans women. We believe in printing on paper, intensive editing, and throwing lots of parties.

REALISTIC

FICTION

anton solomonik

Published by LittlePuss Press, Brooklyn, NY, www.littlepuss.net

This product is GPSR-compliant for sale in the European Union. Authorised Representative: Easy Access System Europe -Mustamäe tee 50, 10621 Tallinn, Estonia, gpsr.requests@easproject.com

LittlePuss

This is a work of fiction. Any resemblance of characters to persons either living or deceased is purely coincidental.

Cover image by Caoimhe Harlock
Cover design by Cat Fitzpatrick
Edited & typeset by Cat Fitzpatrick
Copy-edited by John Sweet

FSC
www.fsc.org

MIX
Paper | Supporting
responsible forestry
FSC® C005010

"How To Run For Local Office While Building a Community out of Nothing" first appeared in *Epiphany Journal*; "The Most Dangerous Game" first appeared in *Evergreen Review*.

ISBN 978-1-7367168-8-5 (print)
ISBN 978-1-7367168-9-2 (e-book)

1 3 5 7 9 10 8 6 4 2

for Jeanne

"There must have been so many soldiers who continually won battles, but got left out of history because they lost their last battle."

— *Reinhard von Lohengramm*

CONTENTS

REALISTIC FICTION

REALISTIC FICTION

I always hated "realistic" fiction. What I mean is slice-of-life-type writing in which it's just people's feelings and observations and no one does anything, there's no plot, no conflict. My father was a scientist, a biologist. He was a hard-working, smart person, and he came to the US on a visa for priority workers, and if he was casually sexist sometimes, it was stupid of me to get upset. For fun, he liked to read police and spy novels. They showed good action and conflict, and a good understanding of the world, crime, and politics.

"It's pure entertainment of course. But oh, there's something to it, you know," he'd tell me.

"I know. I actually agree. I'm not saying I *don't* like it."

"It shows the writer has experienced life. You wouldn't know anything about that!"

"Hahaha," I said. "I do know. I definitely do get it."

I laughed to show him that I was on the same side. I knew how I must have seemed to him. I wasn't trying to fight with him or be different.

After college, I wasn't sure what to do next. I used my father's money to start a hormone regimen and pay for masculinization surgery. My father was initially skeptical, condemning and ridiculing the decision, but after the first few years, even he was satisfied with the physical outcome of the treatment.

As part of the new sense of self I was experiencing from the male hormones, I started to get seriously involved in weightlifting. I even tried to write a short story about it to show my therapist. Though I was trying to avoid the pitfalls of "realistic" fiction, I wanted the plot of this story to reflect what I felt to be the "reality" of weightlifting: the drama of exerting yourself physically against objects, of seeing the effects of this drama on your body and others' bodies. I tried to tie it in with the figure of my father, the way he claimed to have contempt for "aggressive" physical activity, despite his predilection for action-based movies and books.

I kept going to the weightlifting gym. When I showed my therapist the story, she said that she was "not my professor," but that it seemed like the story was very "dense, like I put in a lot of effort." I finished the first phase of the Stronglifts 5x5 program.

Around this time, I went on a date with a woman. I was anxious because I had never done this prior to starting the hormone regimen, and I wondered if I would be able to have, now, a physical and emotional reaction to a person of the, now, opposite sex.

At first, it did not seem like it. Despite the physical changes that had taken place, I found myself experiencing the same interior disconnection. As I walked side by side with her at the art opening, through unheated rooms filled with wire, papier-mâché, plastic, and glass, I felt helpless trying to engage her in dialogue, trying to find things to say about her, me, the art, the weightlifting gym, my story about the weightlifting gym. That same humiliating, feminine instinct to please.

Afterwards, we went to a bar.

"I don't think this is working. I know I said I was bisexual," I said – pretending to be more drunk than I was – "but I think I am actually a gay man."

"What?" she asked, her eyes unfocused.

"I think I am gay. This is more like a friend date. Sorry."

She moved unsteadily on the seat. She thrust her face into mine, touching the upper half of my body.

"You want to be friends??"

"Yes," I answered.

"Are you saying you're not attracted to me?" she asked.

She definitely seemed drunk. She touched my arm. With her other hand, she forced my hand under her shirt.

"You said you were straight," she said, her eyes inches from mine.

I kept my hand under her shirt. The physical contact itself was startling, and not something I had experienced before, but the following sentences, combined with the bodily contact sensation, were what changed the evening for me.

"I'm always alone," she said, "and I spent so much time getting ready for this date. I thought someone like you" – she emphasized *you* – "would get it."

That was when I was able to connect with her on an instinctive level. The way she touched me, without regard for my subjectivity, as if I were an object, an obstacle against which to exert oneself as a result of one's own ridiculous, feminine emotional needs, relieved me of my anxiety and triggered an elemental physical response. "It was like a weight he didn't know he carried was lifted inside him." A phrase from one of my father's police novels. That was how the main character felt after he had sex with a woman.

I pressed my body against hers. "Let's go to my apartment."

We went to my apartment. I shared it with two other guys, trans guys. We squeezed past their bike in the hallway. I pointed out their collection of chunky, oversized sneakers and boots. In my room, the smallest in the apartment, which contained a futon and a water jug that I liked to drink from at night, we had a sexual encounter. I reenacted all the scenes I remembered from mainstream porn, until I wasn't feeling it anymore. We talked afterwards.

"It's cool you have roommates?" she said.

I offered her a drink from the water jug.

"I don't really like them," I told her.

"Well — at least you're not alone, right?"

She tentatively touched my sculpted chest.

I withdrew my hand. I ran it along her neck in another simulation of a porn gesture.

"I'm definitely alone all the time," I told her.

The conversation was reminding me of how I talked to my father. And in fact, seated casually on the edge of the black futon, in the space afforded to me by her lack of awareness of me, her self-loathing, I felt for the first time that I could become my father. If this were a story, here is where the plot would be, I thought. Here would be the beginnings of conflict. I could be anyone, a policeman, a politician. Finally, I was living in reality. I was not living in a "realistic fiction" any more.

MOVING TO BORON

Punk Skunk was working for a woman, Lana Prince, who ran a successful ebook business. She took public domain books and resold them as ebooks. She also maintained several financially remunerative commercial blogs about topics such as travel, small business management, and, even, recursively, commercial blogging. Punk Skunk had a way of not caring about the content of things and therefore managed, I thought, to achieve some success working under her as a freelance blogger and editor.

That's how he got the opportunity to live for free in a house in Boron, CA. She needed him to put fictitious names on some bills and utilities coming into the house, and meanwhile he could keep making money off his old job of smoking e-cigarettes and dashing off jargon-filled marketing emails, reminiscent of his punk poetry in their reliance on free association and neologistic puns, and their abandonment of standard narrative techniques.

It made me kind of jealous that he got that opportunity — I never got an offer like that from any employer I had — but I tried to focus on the positive aspects and see it as an opportunity for myself as well.

"BORON," I said. "I know where that is, dude. I've driven through there when I was taking my brother's car back to his fiancé's place. It is the most starkly compelling and beautiful place to live in America. It is really sublime."

It felt right to speak so flamboyantly, because we had just finished watching another episode of *Sol Invictus*. *Sol Invictus* is an eighties anime in the space opera genre – a retelling of the life of Alexander the Great in the context of a thousand-year-long galactic civil war. The show has an understated yet grandiose tone, filled with scenes in which a Japanese man soberly narrates excerpts of Xenophon and Herodotus while dudes in close-fitting uniforms gaze at each other meaningfully across different tactical maps, and watching it is one of the very few things that makes me feel pure in this world.

I thought about how great it would be to move to Boron. It was so dark when I was driving my brother's car to California, thinking about failure, but in Boron the air had a clean, harsh, chemical smell. Boron is named after the open-pit boron mine that dominates the otherwise featureless landscape. It is 2 miles long and 1.7 miles wide and is the largest open-pit boron mine in the world.

"I am not moving to BORON bro," laughed Punk Skunk.

"WHY NOT bro?" I said. "Do you hate making a decision that's clean and pure?"

"Haha," said Punk Skunk. "There is no way I'm leaving the awesome zine and game dev community here just to go to some town in the middle of nowhere – just to live with my boss!" He wiped his nose with the back of his hand. "Who is not really a person you want to live in the same state as," he added jovially.

"I'll move in with you bro," I interrupted him. "I could get a job at the Boron mine."

"Hahaha."

"I am being serious," I said. "Think about it: You'll save so much money. And you'll be living in the most harsh and brutal place in the world." I furrowed my brows, imparting a heavy, intellectual look to my features. "What happened to your principles?" I asked rhetorically.

"Dude – while I totally appreciate the aesthetics of this decision," said Punk Skunk, "the reality of it is very much not aesthetic. My boss is terrible, and Boron actually sucks."

"It's like you've settled in THIS gentrifying town," I said.

"You're crazy bro."

"I am crazy? I am right. It is like how Alexander totally put Thebes to the sword when he started his military career. Even though it had all that culture that he admired, but he didn't even spare one single life, not even that one symbolic old woman. That is what this is like. Sometimes you gotta put your own shit to the sword. Scorch it in the purifying flames... of Boron."

Punk Skunk thought about my words for a while. A crooked grin spread across his face, exaggerating his naturally asymmetrical features.

"Hahaha," he exclaimed. "Why not?"

5

It took us three days to drive from Austin to Boron. Everywhere I looked, I saw eerie whiteish hills, empty pitiless skies, and endless, sunbaked, boron-rich land. I expressed my enthusiasm for the house in no uncertain terms. It was encircled by a waist-high chain-link fence, with a concrete path leading to a narrow orange front door – a place of mental dedication and pure living. I did not want to go home immediately. I dropped Punk Skunk off at a miniature strip mall to investigate the downtown and immediately drove in the direction of the celebrated mine.

I followed the signs along Borax Road. The long paved highway led to a medium-sized parking lot surrounded by a complex infrastructure of portable buildings, towers, and scaffolding, as if at a construction site. From an aesthetic standpoint, the large, utilitarian-looking compound perfectly complemented the barren landscape in which it stood. But where, I wondered, was the huge hole?

I circled the lot for some time before parking a set distance from what I assumed was the entrance to the vast network of structures. A revolving metal gate said "US Borax Employees Only." I wanted to make it seem like I belonged at the lot, but I did not want Punk Skunk's car to be towed by whatever type of efficient truck they probably used here. A man I hadn't noticed before was approaching the revolving gate.

Finally, I thought. Now, at this moment, life is beginning. Before the man could say anything, I seized the initiative. "I am looking for employment here," I said. "I just moved here."

The man was wearing a white short-sleeved shirt that reflected the hot sun. Its fit suggested a rugged, masculine upper body. He appeared to take in my whole appearance from top to bottom, evaluating my suitability for employment.

"I am an enterprising sort of person," I said quickly. "I have some college-level coursework in several important subjects, including physics and math. I also have a wide array of previous work experience in a variety of sectors."

The man seemed sympathetic, but he made no move to allow me to pass the revolving gate. It is fairly rare, I observed, that a man really looks right in one of those white polo shirts, but this man did. I made a mental note to exercise more when I got back, in hopes of naturally acquiring a similarly erect posture, with no effete curves or unsightly bulges.

"Well, anyway," I continued, "if you have any kind of entry-level work opportunities in either the mine or the boron processing plant, I would be very interested in pursuing those opportunities."

"Huh," said the man. "Sounds good. But this isn't where you apply for a job."

He flashed a confident smile, like a military salute.

"Oh," I said, trying to match the man's practiced, carefree way of talking. "Well, there is a need for me to be on-site."

"Do you have your employee ID?"

"Well, that's the thing. I don't have an employee ID. I am looking for employment."

I stood up straight. "I would like to work in the pit — maybe as a haul truck driver or a drill operator's assistant?" I shrugged in what I hoped was a comradely fashion. "Whatever kind of basic work you have available, really."

The man shook his head. He was not wearing a hat and the sun exaggerated the harsh planes of his face. "This isn't really where you apply for a job."

"Really?" I asked.

I tried to think. Based on my previous experience applying for jobs, I had expected something like this to happen. I went over the various conversational scenarios in my mind, trying to find some psychological trick I could perform. In the parking lot, I found myself strangely lacking in ideas.

"Well, um, do you really believe that?" I said finally.

The man's military smile became slightly less pronounced. "You can go to our website," he said calmly.

"I don't want to go through the website," I began, then stopped.

On a fundamental level, the man did not seem unsympathetic to my plight, but the determination I saw in his eyes was, ultimately, too discouraging. He looked at me, and, I imagined, far beyond me, into the parking lot, into the boron-rich hills. A fighter plane passed overhead. I walked back to Punk Skunk's car, regretting that I had not also worn a polo shirt. Perhaps it would not have improved my chances with the man, but success is all about standing out, making the right gesture.

5

It was four when I drove back to the house. The outside world looked yellow and desaturated, like in an early Playstation 3 shooter. Despite my underwhelming "first job interview" in the parking lot, I had regained that sublime, inspirational feeling. I turned the air conditioner in Punk Skunk's car to its maximum setting and played Beethoven's *Eroica*, which happens to be featured in the opening credits of my favorite space opera anime, *Sol Invictus*.

The front door of the house opened directly into the living room, where Punk Skunk had his laptop set up on the floor. A simple table, made of lightweight wood, stood in the middle of the room. There were no chairs.

"What's up bro," I said.

"Dude's coming to set up the internet tomorrow," said Punk Skunk.

He was smoking an e-cigarette and energetically typing something on his computer – maybe an e-commerce article or one of his incoherent works of punk poetry. This sense of optimistic immersion in many different activities was something I admired about Punk Skunk, even though I found many of his projects to be ill-conceived.

"I am so glad you talked me into it," said Punk Skunk. "Moving here was an AWESOME idea."

"YES," I said.

Punk Skunk kept talking and typing.

"Now I can tell that my vision is truly punk and can persist anywhere."

"The quest for self-improvement starts here," I agreed.

"Hell yes," said Punk Skunk. He grinned from within a cloud of fruit-scented vapor and resumed typing.

My adjustable dumbbells were in a corner of the room, which was otherwise empty besides the laptop and table. I set both of the dumbbells to thirty-five pounds and started doing shoulder presses. I had done five sets of shoulder presses when someone knocked emphatically on the door.

Punk Skunk stopped typing and quickly hid his e-cigarette under his laptop. He opened the door with a flourish, revealing a woman in business casual clothes. It was his boss, Lana

Prince. She looked like a normal businesswoman, wearing a shirt and pants. She shook Punk Skunk's hand. I perceived that she knew him and approved of him as a man and worker.

"Welcome to your new home," she said.

"Thanks, Lana," said Punk Skunk. He addressed her by name. "Thanks for setting this up, you know I don't mind working for ya."

"Yes," I said. I quickly put the dumbbells down. "This is a very efficient home. We will work hard here."

"Hi," said the woman.

"Oh yeah, this is Wolfscum," said Punk Skunk. I frowned in what I thought of as my characteristically intense manner. "Old college classmate and my best friend."

I frowned again. I did not know if Punk Skunk was my "friend," or, maybe, if our friendship could be described in such simple terms, but that was irrelevant. Punk Skunk flashed his asymmetrical grin. Lana Prince now looked like she recognized me.

"That's great," she said. "You're both in law school? Wolfscum is certainly a colorful name."

I had forgotten that Punk Skunk had told his employer he was in law school. I was flattered that he had included me in his career-making lie. I tried to think of some law-related observation I could make later.

"It's 'cause of his penchant for solitude," said Punk Skunk, in response to her second statement.

"That's great," repeated the woman.

That was another of Punk Skunk's traits that I envied — his people skills. His conversation was full of meaningless, if vehement, assertions or, often, outright lies. Yet his unforced, informal manner of speech seemed to inspire confidence in people, despite the frequent incoherence of what he said.

The woman glanced at our utilitarian table and brown, intermittently stained carpet. Our spartan surroundings definitely contrasted with her business casual attire.

"You don't have any furniture," she remarked.

"Nah, I got my laptop, you know that's all the furniture I need!" said Punk Skunk.

"I don't know about that," said the woman. "I brought you guys some chairs. I didn't want to think I was exploiting you in here, ha, ha, ha."

She uttered a sort of spoken laugh.

"That's awesome," said Punk Skunk.

The woman pointed to the desiccated roadway outside.

"We just built a pool and we bought too many chairs," she explained. "There's nowhere to put them now. And we can't resell them— "

"Law," I interrupted her. "I'm actually interested in copyright law. Like, for games."

I immediately regretted my interruption. I did not want Punk Skunk's employer to think I was a so-called "gamer". But fortunately she appeared to be too preoccupied with the chairs to attend to my misstatement.

"Can you two help me?" she insisted.

We went out to her car, which was filled with white plastic chairs. I tried to carry as many chairs as possible back to the house, balancing carefully under the unstable load. Punk Skunk used a different technique to transport the chairs, in which he carried two smaller stacks of chairs, one under each arm. Finally, we finished our task. We were equal in our ability to transport chairs.

The woman cast another appraising glance at our living room, now partly filled with chairs.

"They're outdoor chairs, but you can use them indoors. I just think it would be a huge improvement for you guys."

"Hell yes," said Punk Skunk.

He grabbed one of the chairs and draped himself ostentatiously across its seat.

"Ha, ha, ha," said the woman. "I think I even have a cupholder you can use!"

"No way!" said Punk Skunk. "You don't have to bring it!"

"Oh yes," said the woman. "I'll bring it!"

She returned with a clip-on cupholder, which wobbled slightly when they both tried to install it, but remained attached to the curved armrest. But after the end of the cupholder errand the woman started to look unsure. She stood in the middle of the room, looking around vaguely.

"Would you like a chair?" asked Punk Skunk.

"Yes, thank you."

Punk Skunk put a second chair down on the carpeted floor, and she sat down. I remained standing. I noticed the sun coming in through the western window, creating a silhouette on the opposite wall. It was me.

The woman appeared to relax in the chair. "We got too many of the wrong kind of chairs," she began telling Punk Skunk. "We decided to go with HDPE – much more durable than the molded polypropylene, even given how hot it gets here."

I knew from reading Punk Skunk's articles that HDPE stood for "high-density polyethylene."

"I love the high density plastics," I said.

"Ha, ha, ha," said the woman. She turned back to Punk Skunk. "When we built the pool, I was hoping my daughter would start swimming more. My college-aged daughter?" she reminded him. "Swimming is supposed to be more fun than jogging. But she hasn't been swimming or jogging."

Punk Skunk took out a sheet of crumpled paper and a pencil from the pocket of his punk vest.

"I'm writing all this down," he said.

"Thank you," said the woman.

I stared at my silhouette, with its elongated snout. I wondered if I should have been the one to offer her the chair.

"She needs to take care of her body," continued the woman. She was becoming excited. "She needs to be going out."

"Aw, don't criticize your daughter. I think all body types are valid," said Punk Skunk.

Based on my limited knowledge of Punk Skunk's past activities, in particular with women, I believed that he did not believe that. But his employer did not seem to care.

"Listen," she said. She lightly struck the chair's curved armrest. "We're having lunch tomorrow, you, me, and my daughter. All three of us," she reiterated.

"Writing it down," said Punk Skunk. "It's on my calendar."

"Good," said the woman

He looked up at her. "Is this a business-type lunch?" he asked.

"What do you think?" answered the woman.

She laughed. Then they both laughed.

I glowered by the wall. I could not tell if Punk Skunk's employer was actually displeased with him, or if this was part of an established employer-employee dynamic that I needed to participate in. I thought about what to say.

"There is another branch of the law I'm interested in," I said finally.

The woman turned around. I had moved to the other side of the room while contemplating my shadow, and she now turned to face me.

"I'm interested in workplace safety regulations," I said. "Like at the boron mine?"

I thought about how it is important to try to be personable, to give an impression of mental ease and trustworthiness, in order to achieve mastery over self and others.

"What can I do to find a job at the boron mine? Before," I clarified, "returning to my law studies of course."

5

The next morning, I woke up early. I left Punk Skunk sleeping on the bare mattress in the living room. He looked as lazy and unconcerned in his slumber as he did during his waking hours.

As I had anticipated and feared, the website did not have any jobs, and Lana Prince had also not extended the lunch invitation to include me. However, she had told me that if I knew a lot about boron and borates (and it sounded like I did), I could check out the Borax Visitor Center. She proposed that I investigate the possibility of becoming a docent there. Perhaps that wasn't as glamorous, I thought, as toiling away in the pit, under the pitiless sun, but it could be a reasonable step in the direction of the life I wanted for myself.

The Borax Visitor Center was located on Borax Road. I was encouraged by its proximity to the open-pit mine. Turning off the main road, I maneuvered Punk Skunk's car up a windy, desolate slope and parked in a wide lot. It was almost completely empty except for two boron-related attractions: a replica of a borax-filled wagon hauled by a procession of fiberglass mules (the historic symbol of the town of Boron) and a twelve-foot-tall tire – a real one – from a 240-payload-class mining truck, standing upright at one end of the lot. A low concrete building sat at its other end. Its militaristic, bunker-like appearance comforted me and inspired me with the hope that I was in the right place.

When I opened the door, an older man immediately approached me. He thrust a box into my hand, containing what I already knew to be samples of four different boron-derived minerals.

"This is borax," said the man, with little apparent concern for social preliminaries. "It is also known as sodium borate. These are the boron compounds colemanite, kernite, and ulexite." He pointed to each of the four samples, encased like action figures behind their plastic wrapper.

The man looked like a middle-aged dude in an old Flemish painting. He had close-set eyes and long, thin lips that were very symmetrical and long, thin, vascular hands – probably good at operating many different kinds of boron-extracting machinery. I immediately wanted to show off the internet research I had done on the process of open-pit mining.

"Do you mine them here?" I asked. "The minerals. Also, do you stockpile them after you extract them?"

"What?" said the man.

"The minerals— "

"Oh, yes. We manufacture more than seventeen different varieties of boron-based products."

"That's cool," I said, nodding. The man also nodded. He stood by my side, without continuing the discussion.

I looked around. We were in a large, flourescent-lit room, partly divided by particleboard walls covered with informative posters, photographs, and maps. I saw a poster that showed the six-step process of refining boron: dissolving, settling, crystallizing, filtering, drying, and conveying. I saw a wall dedicated to the display of consumer goods made with boron, which included glassware, detergents, and automotive parts.

I made a few casual circuits of the place. A dude stood next to a scale model of a boron refinery, attending to a small child. The dude – the man – kept trying to get the child to be interested in the model.

"That's where the trucks go," said the man. But the child stared uncomprehending at the miniature structure.

This man must have been the owner of one of the two trucks I had seen parked outside – not 240-payload-class mining trucks, but still trucks. I felt frustrated and jealous. The child looked too old to have had such a dull reaction.

I turned to the first man, the Flemish-faced man. He continued to stand next to the entrance, ready to greet other visitors.

"Listen," I told him. "I am a good worker."

He faced me, unblinking. His icy blue eyes inspired me.

"What I am looking for is a job," I said. "A job in the boron mine. Just a basic, entry-level job, like operating a drill or a blasting apparatus. I have a lot of experience with other entry-level jobs. Of course, I am willing to start by just working here. In this humble place." I waved vaguely at the boron-related exhibits around me. For emphasis, I added a slight, forced laugh.

The man pursed his thin lips. I wondered if he was going to say no.

"Maybe I could assist the person who is operating the drill?" I offered.

The man moved his jaw slowly, without otherwise changing his severe expression. Surely he was a grizzled former miner, a man with no use for anything but the hard practicalities of a situation.

"Do you mean working in the pit?" he asked.

"Yes, exactly," I said, relieved. "I want to work in the pit. Nothing that too many other people would want."

"Well, I can tell you right now you won't find a job in the pit," said the man.

"Oh no."

"You have to be in the union to work in the pit. They put the people on a waiting list and you have to be in the union."

"Oh," I said sadly. I stood uncertainly in front of the man.

"If you want to SEE the pit, on the other hand, there are two places where you can do that," said the man. "If you go down the hall past the men's bathroom, you will see a door to a ramp that will take you to the roof of the building. The other way is I can play you a video about the history of our boron extraction operations. When that's done, it will automatically open our ten-foot-long picture window. Then you can look out of that."

I considered my options. Off to one side, I watched the other man and his child look at a US Borax advertisement from the 1950s.

"I guess I'll watch the video."

The man showed me into the Borax Visitor Center's multimedia room, and I immersed myself in an informative video featuring closeups of borates, drilling machinery, and layers of boron-rich earth. I saw images of people from all walks of life enjoying the different industrial and domestic uses of boron-based products. When the last image faded from the screen, the curtains on the other side of the auditorium parted and I approached the ten-foot-long window.

I looked down and at last I saw it – the ridged and terraced hole dropping down only a few feet away from the other parking lot, the one on which I had been driving just the previous day. Enormous trucks, each one possessing six 12-foot tires like the one I had seen outside the Borax Visitor Center, wound their way up and down the mine's blasted sides. Though I was looking at it from behind a wall of UV-protective glass, it felt like I was right there. It was inspiring. It was exactly like the pictures I had seen of it on the internet.

At some point, while I was looking at the mine, the Flemish-faced man came and stood beside me. He and I stood alone, separately regarding the uncanny panorama. He broke the silence.

"See those tan-colored hills over there? That is overburden from the mine. It is the excess rock that lies above the ore. You can distinguish the overburden from the colemanite that we stockpile."

I gazed down at the pit. "You need an assistant docent," I said passionately.

The Flemish-faced man said nothing. "Someone to show people around, do extra work, anything," I said. "Not many people want that work. But I will be that man."

The man remained silent for some time. But maybe the sight of this massive edifice affected him. We both looked down at it – the vertiginous hole, a man-made Grand Canyon, far more evocative than the real Grand Canyon. He finally spoke.

"If you're looking for something to do, come see me tomorrow."

"Oh, wow. That is great news," I breathed.

The man looked at me. He seemed to be really seeing me for the first time, observing and appraising my specific features with eyes that were a cold, light blue. "There are not many people who want this work. It is because I don't think I can pay you. But who knows?" he mused.

"Maybe it can transition into paid work," I said eagerly.

"Sure. Maybe." He paused. "You will learn the right way to coil a length of cable working for me, I can tell you that," he concluded.

I stood next to the man. I continued to gaze at the hole beyond the glass. Finally, I took my leave of the man. I left the multimedia room and climbed to the viewing area on the roof. Below me lay the slope leading directly into the open-pit mine. A sign read: "Final Slope: Do Not Disturb."

By the railing, I saw the dude from before, accompanied by the passive child. I watched him walk away from the viewing area with the child and descend into a car that had just pulled into the parking lot – a different car, not one of the two parked trucks. The Flemish-faced man must have owned both of the trucks. I turned away from the now-irrelevant scene and looked at the desert, exposing my face to the scorching winds.

⌒

"I can't believe it!" I told Punk Skunk later that day. We were sitting on the white chairs Lana Prince had given us and watching *Sol Invictus* on his laptop. "I actually got a job in Boron!"

"Bro," said Punk Skunk. "That's great news bro."

He took a satisfied drag on his e-cigarette. He took a sip of some pumpkin-flavored beer that he had put in the attached cupholder on his chair. We were watching the story arc that dealt with assassination attempts. Alexander knew that one of the eight fleet admirals was going to make an attempt on his life. Everyone knew that he knew – but Ptolemy, due to his reputation for reason and caution, was above suspicion. Yet it was precisely Alexander's trust in Ptolemy's "reason," which Ptolemy considered a form of contempt, that made him determined to kill one of his closest personal friends.

I took a sip of my own beer, which was an amber ale (we had bought a sampler pack), as I savored this nuanced portrayal of male relationships. I picked up and put down one of the adjustable dumbbells with my foot, doing sets of ten reps.

"What was the job?" asked Punk Skunk.

"Only in Boron can a man just drive into town and immediately find honest employment," I answered.

In the semidarkness of the room filled with chairs, in the context of these animated scenes of noble dudes conquering a vast cosmic emptiness, my experience at the Visitor Center seemed transfigured. The endless conversations with the Flemish-faced man, the meandering circuits of the same walls covered with informative posters — all began to seem like part of a larger, majestic narrative arc.

"Awesome that you have a job," replied Punk Skunk. "Now you can stop living off your brother and his family. You can even save up money to do something cool!"

"I don't just live off my brother," I protested. "I have had jobs before."

"Hey, I don't care if you live off your brother or not," said Punk Skunk. "You know my philosophy bro. I just thought it would be interesting if you used the money on something."

"Oh, what, like make a zine? Buy a lot of e-cigarette refills?" I waved away Punk Skunk's fruit-scented vapor. "Art is the refuge of weaker men. The best art acknowledges that."

On the screen, two admirals clinked goblets together against the background of a starry void.

"Art must complement action," I clarified.

"Wolfscum, you are one weird dudebro," said Punk Skunk.

"And besides, I won't have money at first," I added. "I am not getting paid right away. I am just getting my foot in the door."

"Hm," said Punk Skunk, skeptically.

He actually looked slightly concerned – an uncharacteristic look for him.

"You don't understand," I said. "Nobody understands."

I did not want to continue talking like this. On the screen, the scene with the admirals faded out.

"Listen – let me tell you about my day," said Punk Skunk, finally changing the subject.

He told me about the lunch he had had with Lana Prince. According to Punk Skunk, his employer was pleased with him. She was pleased with the speed with which he wrote SEO articles and crafted fake ebooks. And she really had brought her daughter to the lunch. She wanted Punk Skunk to manage a team of other content creators, and she also wanted him to date her daughter.

"What does this have to do with what we were talking about before?" I asked. As I mentioned earlier, I was envious of the respect Punk Skunk commanded from his employer, but I did not want to outwardly signal this fact.

"Nothing," said Punk Skunk. "I was just thinking, maybe you should hang out with that girl instead of me. She seems like someone you would like – sort of serious and boring."

"Oh, I see," I laughed. "Haha."

I started to play the next episode of *Sol Invictus*. It featured a battle against a planet-sized golden space-fortress (held in place by six ranks of neoclassical caryatids), depicted from the point of view of each of the eight fleet admirals in turn. "Man's immortality is not to live forever; but each moment free from fear makes a man immortal," said Alexander. I picked up the adjustable dumbbells. I thought about doing shoulder presses.

꒜

I stayed up for a long time that night, weightlifting, talking to Punk Skunk, thinking about the future. I left early next morning. I drove through Boron in Punk Skunk's sensible car, not using the air-conditioning, enjoying the bracing, sulfurous smells of the desert wafting in through the open windows. I flattered myself with the belief that I was already becoming a hard man, ground down by relentless labor in the hot sun.

The Flemish-faced man greeted me in the same place as yesterday. The two white pickup trucks were still parked outside.

"Now you are here," said the man.

"You own both trucks?" I asked.

"Yes. One is for power tools and lumber. One is for my personal use."

I was wearing business casual pants made from a sturdy fabric, which could be used for moderate physical activity. I wore a polo shirt, and so did the Flemish-faced man — mine was gray and his was maroon. I wore a sweatband on my forehead. I had been worried the man would frown upon this accessory, or think it was frivolous or unneeded, but he did not seem to notice it.

We walked past the exhibits (there were now no visitors) and into a side door behind the gift shop. We ended up in a room with a concrete floor. There were power tools and construction supplies all over the floor. The man looked at a clipboard that hung from his pants.

"You know your way around a set of tools?" he asked.

"Definitely," I answered.

The man moved his tongue in his mouth, as if trying to dislodge an imaginary object. He shook his head. "You do any project," he said, "you have got to do it right. Start it right."

"Hmm," I said respectfully.

The man looked at his clipboard. "I have been working and building for more than thirty years. Working and building. Building and working. This I will tell you," said the man.

I adjusted my sweatband.

"All your tools need to be in the right place. All your cable needs to be in the right place. All your lumber needs to be in the right place. You must do the whole job," said the man. "From the beginning."

"Right," I said. "You can't cut corners when you are working."

"You can't cut corners when you are working," repeated the man. "You must do the whole job. And if you skip a step, that will be reflected in the outcome. That's how people will see your work. As the work of someone who doesn't work. Does that make sense?"

"Yes," I said "That makes sense."

"And, therefore, when you do work," continued the man, "before you get started working" – he gestured at the floor – "you must document the tools that you have to work with. And that's the first thing that you'll be doing for me."

With a flourish, he showed me the contents of his clipboard. It was a printed spreadsheet with a list of construction tools and materials: wrenches, ratchets, sockets, two-by-fours, and other such items.

"These are all the tools and materials we have at the Borax Visitors Center. These are all the tools and materials I have. Before you get started, you have to document the tools that you have," he reiterated.

I readjusted my sweatband, disoriented by his repetitive words. He handed me the clipboard. "Look at this spreadsheet," he continued. "Now look at the floor." I looked at the floor. "If you see something on the floor, it will be documented on this spreadsheet. If it is not on the floor, it does not belong on the spreadsheet. And take initiative," he enjoined. "If it is on the floor and it is not on the spreadsheet – you add it to the spreadsheet. Write it down." He shook the clipboard's attached pencil.

With those final instructions, the man ambled over to a barren patch of floor near the wall, stepping over several tarp-covered mounds. He crossed his arms and began to watch me work. I nodded. I looked at the floor again. There certainly were a lot of objects on the floor.

I sat on a piece of cardboard. I carefully arranged my limbs on the shifting, unstable material. I decided to focus on a clear plastic bag filled with ball bearings and brackets. I counted the ball bearings and put them in another bag that had been lying near the original bag. I was separating the ball bearings from the brackets. This took some time. I realized that I had misplaced the clipboard with the spreadsheet. I was worried I would not be able to count the ball bearings without the spreadsheet. I suddenly felt a hand descend on my shoulder – strong, yet brittle. It was that man. He had come back over.

"Don't sit like that," said the man. "It is slowing you down."

He put his hands under my armpits. I stood up, partly lifted off the ground by the man's thin, powerful arms.

"You get the work done a lot faster if you are on your feet," said the man. "Like this." He assumed kind of squatting position, with his pelvis high in the air and his feet on the floor.

I watched him squat next to me on the cardboard, his maroon-shirted back perfectly rigid. I tried to imitate him. The position was similar to the bent-over barbell row exercise for your back, except that it did not feel empowering. The man stood up to critique my position. "Do not curve your spine," he warned.

"I wasn't curving my spine."

"You will get back problems that way," said the man. He put his hands on my chest and back, correcting the perceived flaws in my posture. The physical contact was firm, yet impersonal. I kept my head facing forward, so that he could see I was following his directions. Moving only my eyes, I saw the clipboard with the spreadsheet. I reached for it, just as he let go of my body. "Okay. Now you won't get back problems," he said.

"Thanks." I remained in the squatting position as I watched the man step away from me. He observed me for a few moments, then turned around. He assumed his own squat in different corner of the room. I continued to organize the ball bearings. We were both working.

After some time had passed, the man returned. I had finished counting the ball bearings from the initial bag, and had started on a new bag. I felt the man's eyes on me, but remained in the squatting position, despite the slight strain in my quads.

"Keep your back straight," said the man.

"Okay."

Again, he began to manually adjust my posture. Then, suddenly, he released me.

"Wait a minute," he said.

He picked up the new bag of ball bearings. He held it up to the light streaming in from the room's high windows, peering up at it with Biblical wonder.

"You've just been putting these roller bearings right back where you found them," he said slowly. "You have been look‑ ing at the tools. You haven't been organizing the tools."

"No way, I've been organizing the tools," I protested. I didn't want him to think I was doing a bad job. "I've been putting them in two separate bags. Look."

I showed him my work. I had two separate bags for, respectively, ball bearings and brackets.

The man shook his head. "You have been working for me for this past half-hour. But you haven't been WORKING. Do you understand the difference?"

"I think so?"

I wondered if I should still remain in the bent-over position.

"No," said the man. "What I mean is that you've been working, but you haven't been applying the information you have been given."

He squatted alongside me. He glanced at the clipboard. Then, unconcerned with the clipboard, he emptied out all the bags I had worked on, as well as several more nearby bags, and began to sort. Moving with frightening efficiency, he began to organize the items from the bags into piles separated by size, shape, and function.

"You've just been doing the work you were given like a machine," he said. "You can't do this job if you're just going to be a machine."

Moving only my eyes, I watched as the man continued to sort objects in the bent-over position, impressed by his speed and attention to detail. There was nothing for me to do except watch. He moved so quickly. I wondered if I would ever be able to achieve the same mastery over space and objects.

"So," I asked after a while, just to say something, "how long have you lived in Boron?"

"Did you say something?"

"Have you lived here a long time?"

"You haven't been listening," said the man, still without stopping what he was doing. "I have been working and building for more than thirty years."

"Oh," I said.

He did not say anything else. I finally stopped squatting. Then the only sound was the occasional shuffle of cardboard on concrete as the man continued to rearrange various tools and fasteners. It was a humbling sound – the sound of someone else working without regard for anyone who might be standing by or observing. I thought about the desert and tried to purge myself of emotions.

҂

I came back to find Punk Skunk in the front yard, talking to someone. It was a girl. Based on the girl's appearance and posture, I could discern immediately that it was Punk Skunk's employer's daughter – the one who was "serious and boring" in a way supposedly reminiscent of myself. I kicked open the gate in the miniature chainlink fence. I had spent more than eight hours at Borax Visitor Center organizing tools, listening to the criticisms of the man.

"Hey dudes," I said, trying to not seem serious.

"Nice moves," said Punk Skunk.

"Thanks. Let's go on a walk," I said quickly.

"Haha, sure, a walk could be chill," said Punk Skunk. "A 'brief constitutional.' You would probably call it that," he asserted.

He grinned mischievously.

"This is Wolfscum, by the way," he told the daughter.

"I am Wolfscum," I confirmed for her benefit.

"Haha, so I've heard," said the daughter.

She had short hair with the tips dyed blue. She wore a tan trenchcoat and cargo pants with multiple pockets. I could see why Punk Skunk though she was similar to me. She talked as if reenacting the stylized dialogue of fictional characters. I had also been told I talked this way.

"That's good. Lots of people have heard of me," I said.

"Oh, really? Why?" said the daughter.

"That was a joke. I was being sarcastic."

"I could tell you were joking," said the daughter unconvincingly. "I was going along with the joke."

She smiled cautiously. We looked at each other. I frowned in response to her apparent discomfort with my wolf-like glower.

"Okay, so let's go!" said Punk Skunk. "You know I actually got somewhere to be in Boron."

"We all do," I said.

Punk Skunk laughed at my statement.

Without changing out of my work clothes, I jumped over the miniature chain-link fence. Punk Skunk and the daughter followed me. We walked down the empty street. The late afternoon sun made everything look orange. We made inconsequential statements and comments.

When we got to Twenty Mule Team Road, Punk Skunk stopped.

"Sorry," he said. "I gotta go in that Mexican restaurant."

"Okay," I said.

Despite myself, I looked to the daughter for guidance.

"I gotta take care of some things in there," he chuckled.

Then he strode across the parking lot, without waiting for a response. He disappeared inside the restaurant.

"Should we follow him?" I suggested to the daughter.

The daughter did an exaggerated shrug.

"No?" I said. "Okay," I said uncertainly. "Let's keep walking."

We continued to walk along Twenty Mule Team Road. We passed a gas station, a thrift store, and another twelve-foot-tall mining truck tire, similar to the one at the Borax Visitor Center. The daughter took surprisingly big strides. She was actually a fast walker.

"That restaurant was where we all had lunch yesterday," said the daughter. "My mom is always taking me there for lunch."

"Wow," I said, trying to make conversation.

"She is always asking the servers if I look fat," said the daughter.

I wondered if she wanted me to say, "I don't think you look fat." I did not know if I thought that. She did not look worse than most women.

"Oh. That is why you did not want to go in the restaurant?" I said finally.

"No! Well, kind of. But no." She hunched over as she walked, as if bracing against the slight, sulfurous breeze. "I kind of think he wanted to go there alone," she said.

"That's fine. Nothing wrong with that," I told her.

She looked down. "One of the people talked to him when we were there with my mom. Maybe the bartender? She told him to 'stop by later' for 'free margaritas.' Well, I don't remember what she said exactly. But I think she was flirting. With 'Punk Skunk'. Like when my mom wasn't looking."

She looked at me, as if to gauge my reaction.

"What? You don't know that!" I said.

We walked past an American Legion post and a few small parking lots. This part of the street had sidewalks and we walked on the sidewalks.

"That's what you think?" I asked indignantly. "That he went in the restaurant to flirt with the bartender or whatever?!"

We approached Boron Avenue. I turned instinctively, not caring where I was going.

"Well, maybe," I conceded. "He is very conventional in a lot of ways. Despite being named Punk Skunk."

"Haha," the daughter laughed rhetorically. "I guess I don't notice if people are conventional or unconventional."

We walked by a few dirt lots and houses. I saw a Joshua tree. I saw a building that was maybe a school. Suddenly, the sidewalk ended. We departed the downtown strip and entered the open desert, walking along the side of the straight road. The daughter shielded her eyes with her hand. We walked for several minutes in silence.

"Ugh, I just hate the sun!" said the daughter. "Sometimes I wish everything could be shrouded in darkness."

The sun was now very low in the sky. It created dramatic shadows over the shrub-covered landscape. She laughed nervously.

"Well, yeah, it will be dark soon," I said lamely.

I suddenly felt demoralized. I was still wearing my sweatband from the job. I recalled the specifics of my day with that man, how he showed me the correct posture for coiling cables and organizing tools, the confident way he held objects. Despite the salutary effects of the boron extraction by-product smell from the refinery, I felt a wave of nausea.

"Um, are you okay?" asked the daughter.

She stood above me. I saw that she wore a belt over her cargo pants, with belt loops that held multiple objects and pouches.

"Yes," I said. "I'm fine."

"You don't seem okay. You're just sitting on the ground."

She unhooked a reusable water bottle from one of her belt loops and offered it to me.

I assessed that it would only show weakness if I looked unsure or refused her offer. I drank the water. It had a warm, metallic taste. I could imagine drinking out of a similar bottle at work during brief rest intervals.

"It actually is refreshing. Thanks," I said.

"No problem. You can easily get dehydrated walking around like this."

The daughter took out a camouflage-print bucket hat from one of her cargo pants pockets.

"I have a lot of different survival gear in here," she said.

"What? Sorry. It's just that I hate my job."

I continued to sit on the ground.

"Oh," said the daughter. She spoke in a slightly subdued tone. She looked at the hat, but did not put it on.

"I still think the sun is bad," she said. "We both should have worn hats."

"They're not even paying me," I told her. I tried to make it into a speech. "Not that it would matter. I have already borrowed too much, given up too much. There is nothing I can do to cleanse the corruption in terms of money."

The daughter put away the hat.

"I guess that makes sense. My parents are paying for my college, and that's embarrassing," she offered.

I closed my eyes. "I do not want much in this life," I said. "I do not want a zine or a car or possessions. I just want to have a good life, filled with hard work and the cold satisfaction of self-mastery."

I contemplated the vastness of the desert. I thought of the hole. I stood up.

"It's just so humiliating," I said finally.

"I can relate to feeling humiliated," the daughter said earnestly. She looked pleased that we were both standing.

To distract myself, I looked at some low hills on the horizon. I experienced a happy recognition. Even here, far from any explanatory placards, I could perceive that they were overburden from the boron mine, due to their tan color (which looked orange in the setting sun) and characteristic 30 percent grade.

"Wow, look at those hills," I said.

"That's overburden from the mine," said the daughter.

5

We decided to walk towards the overburden. During this part of the walk, we started talking about ourselves. The daughter said that she lived at home and went to Barstow Community College in Barstow. She liked music, movies, and watching shows. Her mom said she wasn't applying herself in life or college.

"She says I should not be so depressed all the time. She says I am making my life depressing."

"Yes, its important to not be too serious and boring."

"I guess so," she admitted. "Well, I'm in the anime club at college."

I did not say anything.

"That's something not serious about me," she clarified.

"Yes, that is non-serious."

I repeated what I had told her before about my life. I said that I was looking for a job in Boron. I did not know what she would be able to say to that statement. But before she could fail to reply, we arrived at a rusted barrier gate that blocked the rest of the road. Beyond it, I saw the overburden – a vast mound of limestone, gypsum, and other by-products of boron mineral extraction, as tall as a city building. Any vehicle could easily go around the gate. It had a purely symbolic function.

"Wow, we can get to the top!" I said, with real enthusiasm.

"You're not supposed to walk on the overburden," said the daughter. But she ran after me.

I yelled at her. "We must seek high elevation!"

She laughed in what seemed like a non-rhetorical way – moved, perhaps, by my actual excitement. I began to run up the side of the crumbling mass.

I did not get far. I quickly stopped, out of breath, to dislodge the jagged shards of limestone and gypsum that filled my non-slip dress shoes. I looked down at the daughter, who was following me up the slope.

She had put on the camouflage-print hat. By this point the sun had gone down, so it was probably no longer necessary for sun protection. Despite the daughter's flawed personal style, improperly reminiscent of a shonen anime protagonist, the sight of a solitary figure in a loose coat was, nonetheless, striking in the twilight. She quickly caught up to me on the rocky ascent.

"Looks like you're wearing more practical shoes than me," I said.

"These army boots come in handy," she agreed. "Well, handy for your feet."

I removed more loose shards from my shoes. She kept climbing. I watched the back of her trench coat, with its specific, possibly flawed proportions, get smaller along the 30 percent grade.

"Did you ever play girls field hockey and stuff?" I asked.

She stopped, sending down a cascade of overburden.

"Um, my mom made me play volleyball in high school?"

"Oh," I said. "Because you are going pretty fast. I thought you didn't like jogging or sports."

"I don't think I like organized sports! Or jogging."

"Well, I did a lot of sports," I lied. "When I was in law school."

I did not want to appear to be as behind her as I was, so I attempted to make her wait for me by continuing the conversation.

"I liked the competitive aspect of sports," I said, hurrying upwards. "How else are you supposed to relate to other people, unless you are trying to best them in some sort of physical or mental conflict?"

The daughter looked down.

"I guess it wasn't like that for me."

"That's stupid," I said. "That is how men relate to each other. Maybe women are different, even non-stereotypical women."

But I was out of breath again. The daughter resumed her rapid movement up the overburden and did not answer. By the time we got to the top, the sky was almost purple. She looked over at the other side of the colossal mound. "There's the boron mine," she said.

When I finally dragged myself up to where she was standing, I saw what she was looking at. Even in the dim light, I could easily perceive the vast size of the open-pit mine, the jagged indentations it made in the earth. I saw the refinery, a toy-like structure to the west. I saw the Borax Visitor Center, where I had spent so much of the day, dwarfed by the open-pit mine below. I saw the mine's sixteen concentric terraces, encircling the barely visible bottom of the hole, where shovels and explosives extracted boron ore during the daytime operational hours, and maybe also sometimes at night.

"Wow," I said. "It's like the Grand Canyon."

"I hate looking at it," said the daughter.

"No way. I think its inspiring."

"It's just so" – she paused for effect – "depressing and mundane at the same time."

"No way," I repeated.

I kept looking at the pit. As it got darker, the pit and the sky became less differentiated from each other.

"Sorry for being so melodramatic," said the daughter. "I know the US Borax mine creates a lot of jobs. And its not as bad for the environment as coal mining and stuff..."

I continued to look down.

"There are so many worlds, and I have not yet conquered even one," I said with suppressed emotion.

"Oh my god! That's a quote from that show!" said the daughter.

"Yes..." I said warily.

I should not have been surprised that she might have watched other anime, aside from the typical shonen content.

"Oh my god," repeated the daughter. "I don't know anyone who watches that show. It's so good."

She looked at me. I saw it in my peripheral vision. She sighed, enraptured. I kept looking down. I could no longer see the bottom of the pit.

"And it always makes me feel safe somehow," she added. "No matter how bad things get, Alexander and Hephaestion will always be there for each other."

Her tone, so earnest and unironic, finally made me look at her directly. She was still wearing the camouflage-print bucket hat. Her face looked monochromatic in the growing darkness. Almost like an anime character, but not quite.

"Hm," I said, embarrassed.

"Sorry, I'm probably saying too much," said the daughter.

I looked back at the hole, at the undifferentiated purple void where I knew the hole to be. I suddenly felt cold, disdainful. I thought of that man at the Borax Visitor Center, waiting for me every day. I was ready.

Finally, I thought. The thing I wanted this whole time. The purifying flame, the cold satisfaction of self-mastery.

"I don't know why I said that. I definitely don't watch that show," I told her.

"Oh," said the daughter.

The sweatband was on my forehead, the keys to Punk Skunk's car in my pocket. It was almost the last episode, I realized. After the battle of the eight admirals, Alexander's empire was going to collapse from within.

THE MEETING OF MINDS

I was nineteen when I met up with the Ayn Rand guy.

"Hi, I'm Geoff," he said.

I knew his name, and how it was spelled, because it was in his email address. By contrast, my emails to him said they came from "Don Ferdinand of Austria" – the name of a Habsburg emperor from the 1800s. It was intended as an ironic reference.

He shook my hand.

"Hi," I said.

"Excited to finally meet you."

He was much taller than me. He had a long face with a big chin and glasses. I was surprised by how much taller he was than me.

"Yes, I am also excited," I said, trying to modulate my voice appropriately.

He asked me how I was doing.

"Okay."

"Good."

"Yes," I said.

I suspected this was not going to work. He moved slightly closer to me. Maybe I had just imagined it. I tried again.

"But no, okay is actually good! It's neutral, which is good. Emotions are not a tool of cognition," I quoted — a phrase used repeatedly in Ayn Rand's essays and novels.

"Haha," he acknowledged.

He turned so we were fraternally side by side.

We started walking towards the student parking lot. It was a bright, sunny day with a slight breeze.

"It's so awesome to find someone like you who goes to this school," he said.

"Yes," I agreed.

I knew what he meant.

"Someone articulate who is really familiar with Objectivism, and classical liberalism, and these ideas."

"That's me!"

Geoff (he had a last name, as I also knew from his email address) had found my name in our college's student directory. My entry had a picture of me in a Victorian brocade dress, with links to my various social media accounts and websites, including my Reddit account and my post history in the old "Rebirth of Reason" forums. We had exchanged several long emails over the past two weeks, talking about Ayn Rand and what we both liked about her, which of her books we had read.

He put his hands in the pockets of his peacoat.

"I definitely like Ayn Rand," I said.

He laughed again.

"Yes, you mentioned."

We walked past the life sciences building. I glanced at the gap between the life sciences building and the campus bookstore, where I had once stopped to eat a Popsicle I had bought from the student store. I remembered how the world had seemed to me then – the texture and taste of the frozen fruit, the concrete slabs holding up the roof of the building. I had felt, then, fully rational in my individual consciousness, capable of "perceiving the universe with the fearless eagerness of a child, knowing it to be intelligible" (as Ayn Rand had put it in *For the New Intellectual*).

We entered the school parking lot. I decided to end the "small talk."

"So let's say we say something is a chair," I began. I gestured at a car. "Suppose we say that is a chair."

He looked at the car, but didn't answer. I tried to situate my words in their context.

"So I agree with Ayn Rand's – ethics, I guess? That's what I'm trying to say. It's just the specifics of her worldview that I'm unsure of."

"You guess," he said with a slight smile. He was looking at me now, not the car. "But sure. Which specifics?"

His height, his physical presence, with its unmistakable connotation of a date, were disconcerting – but maybe it was fine. Maybe it still was plausible, this meeting of minds.

"Well, so, Objectivism would say this 'chair'" – I pointed at the car again – "exists 'out there', independently of us perceiving it."

He thought about it. "Well, yes," he said. "Reality exists whether you want it to or not."

"Yes, but." I avoided his eyes. I gestured at the air above the car.

What did I like about Ayn Rand? What was it I liked about her ethics?

"If I say, 'this is a brown chair', where do those concepts reside?" I asked. "Aren't 'brown' and 'chair' human mental constructs?"

He looked at me. The car was not brown.

"No," he said. "I disagree. A chair is a *concept*, yes." He began to lecture. "Our minds create concepts to group similar physical entities. But those entities exist in reality. That's how we reason about reality. That's how we have logic, and science."

"No, that's not it, we can still have logic and science," I said quickly.

I caught myself making an unsure, grasping gesture. What was it I had written?

"Can't we say that we group certain *perceptions*," I said, making the gesture again, "as being *related to chairs* because that is in our *interest* to do so, as humans? So we say certain things are 'brown'" – I squinted at the car – "because that allows us to conceive of how our eyes perceive, uh" – I paused – "light reflecting off objects or something. Yes," I went on. I knew what I wanted to say. "And it can be taken back another step. We say 'light' because that is how it is useful to us to conceive of *seeing* and *vision*. We are following our will – our specific, rational, individual consciousness as men, as humans."

Geoff studied my face. He shook his head, which was a full head above me.

"No," he said. "Objects have an essence, sure, but its just those traits that make them what they are. Aristotle talks about this. You drive a car. You sit in a chair. It's not about words, wants, whims, wishes, or perceptions."

"Yes," I said. I tried not to look at him. I had notebooks full of diagrams that said things like "constraint" and "humility versus power." "But what are *objects*?" I asked finally. "What constitutes *objects*?"

"Objects are what you can perceive."

He closed the physical distance between us. His face had specific attributes and traits. I was silent.

"You're overthinking this," he said. "You're trying to make relativism work. Relativism is boring."

He actually touched my shoulder.

"Have you read *Introduction to Objectivist Epistemology*?"

"Uh, no? Maybe?" I found it hard to talk.

"It's good," he said. "She gets into formal philosophy."

"Wow."

What did I like about Ayn Rand? I had read several of her books: *The Fountainhead*, *Anthem*, *For the New Intellectual*. They had relatable characters who rose above their bland milieu, and who shared my philosophical discomfort with "small talk." They addressed metaphysical and ethical questions about consciousness, art — buying and selling art on the free market. They asked if there really was an axiom, a "first principle" from which you could know things, true things, about the world, using reason. They imparted a feeling of clarity that was missing from this conversation — a call to ignore one's immediate world, the false world, with its unreasonable demands, its brutal, consensus interpretations.

Geoff began to recite. "In *Introduction to Objectivist Epistemology*, she explains how concepts are formed at the perceptual level through a process of differentiation and integration. We perceptually discriminate and discern among certain entities in the world, seeing them as apart from each other and from their backgrounds. So then concepts are neither *intrinsic*, abstract entities existing independently of a person's consciousness, *nor* subjective hallucinations. Concepts are *objective*," he concluded, "in an epistemological sense — because they reflect reality."

"Uh," I said. I was aware of my body language, my cringing gestures. "So I guess its a question of whether those... qualities of entities on the basis of which we form concepts exist in the mind or" — I wasn't sure what to say — "somewhere inside those entities," I conceded.

"You can't say a car is a chair." He smiled slightly.

I was not opposed to having sex, in theory. In Ayn Rand's novels, characters with compatible philosophical views were immediately compelled to have violent, urgent, passionate sex — especially if the characters were opposite sex, of course (and this particular situation, of course, seemed to suggest that outcome) but not necessarily. It was easy to imagine Ayn Rand as gay, as having sex with a philosophically compatible woman. Sex was the logical outcome of two characters' metaphysical compatibility.

"Okay," I said, not moving away from him.

I had said on the internet that arguing about definitions was the highest form of activity in life.

"You know, you're different than I thought you would be," said Geoff after a while.

"I am?"

"You're a lot quieter."

He smiled. He had a full set of large teeth, proportionate to his height.

"You don't exist," I said finally.

"What?"

"You really don't exist," I felt compelled to repeat.

He looked surprised to hear my statement. "Are you citing a thought experiment?"

I kicked him in the shin, briefly evoking a vivid childhood memory.

Then I turned and quickly walked away, and did not stop until I was on the other side of the campus.

I saw that he had not followed me. Should I delete his emails or block him on the internet? I put the question out of my mind. It did not belong to the part of the universe that was intelligible.

After a few hours had passed, I went to the student store. It was still open. I purchased my second Popsicle of the semester. It was so red that it looked as if it was made out of meat, and it actually contained frozen chunks of real berries.

HOW TO RUN FOR LOCAL OFFICE WHILE BUILDING A COMMUNITY OUT OF NOTHING

Ashton felt excited and worried when his OkCupid friend, Chris, started to put his hand on his leg. Finally the time had come for the sexual part of their interaction together.

There had been a whole conversation they had had earlier in the pizza place and on the long, ambiguous walk along Bedford Avenue, in which Ashton had tried to impress upon Chris the significance of his life, its development: all those times after school in high school, sitting on the curb at Jack in the Box all day; the time he lived in an apartment complex in Texas and watched an anime series about *hikikomori* and why he liked it so much; the other time he watched an anime series about Alexander, the space emperor, and why that was important; and now, the most recent development: He was going to run for political office in Brooklyn or Queens. And he wasn't just going to run for the city council, or state

58

assembly, or any of the typical first steps one would expect. No. He was planning to get his name on the ballot for the Democratic primary for the 2018 US House elections.

Ashton had heard from Dan — this dude that he sort of knew — that Carolyn Maloney, who had served for thirteen consecutive sessions as the representative for the 14th and 12th districts (parts of Manhattan, Queens, and Brooklyn), was going to step down. Together, he and Dan had strategized that, maybe, in the ensuing power vacuum, it would be possible for Ashton to raise money and awareness for himself as the state's first, and the country's third, transgender congressional candidate.

As Ashton was describing these political goals, his hair had flopped playfully over his eyes and he'd gestured a little, trying to derive from his date's placid face the inspiration he had felt earlier last week in the park, talking to Dan and some other people in that group.

"I'd be the perfect figure for these, like — troubled times or whatever," Ashton had said to Chris. "Kind of like a member of a disadvantaged group, but not. Kind of like a white male, but not. Outwardly and aesthetically conservative but with actual progressive values. Or maybe the other way around, I can't tell, hahaha."

Chris had laughed at this. "So you're running as a bit?"

"Well, no!" said Ashton. He hated hearing that expression "Well, I mean yeah, I guess I get why people would say that. Like its cynical. But I can *use* my pettiness and just sort of shitty cynicism to do something good for once, hahaha."

Chris had looked at Ashton, genial and concerned, like a blond dad (he was blond), like someone who had grown up in a family with dogs (he had told Ashton that he had). "Ashton," he said. He paused. "If you're trying to do something good, you don't need to be all *sad* and negative about it you know. You can just say you're trying to do something good."

He patted him on the back, slightly critical and yet, perhaps, also interested and intrigued by Ashton's complex, self-aggrandizing personality. This was on the walk to Chris's apartment. Feeling the hand on his back, this casual erasure of the physical barrier, Ashton felt simultaneously excited and almost reassured. He thought for the first time that maybe this date would be successful or at least tolerable.

Now they were in the apartment. It was on the top floor of a two-story house Chris was renting with his partner and two cats (his parents back home had dogs, but he and his partner had cats). Chris led Ashton into a small, windowless room, which he informed Ashton served as his "office." He put his hand on Ashton's leg while they sat on a futon, which was positioned across from a desk with two large monitors. Chris was a 3D animator for a games studio that made free-to-play online games. His partner was a developer at a different games studio. As they began to touch one another in a consensual manner, Ashton felt that his excitement was possibly a sexual one, though maybe it was not.

Chris was self-aware to an acceptable degree, a nice person who valued niceness. His partner, in addition to his work as a developer, maintained the servers for the Working Families Party of the State of New York. It was this potential, if tenuous, connection to the state's most influential left-wing third party that was the reason Ashton was on this OkCupid date in the first place.

Ashton started making out with Chris. He felt the spit in his mouth, that same illicit feeling he remembered when, years ago, he was made to hold a boy's hand during middle school square dancing; when, several years before that, at a summer camp, he had gotten in trouble after fellating some older boys. The idea, both exciting and isolating, that you could go to this unfamiliar place with people. It was supposed to be such a private and special thing – he remembered hearing this in his health class – but you could go there literally with anyone, with any random person.

"Your mouth tastes like that gum you chew," said Chris. "It's nice."

"Oh, uh, thank you," said Ashton. He wondered if Chris liked him, if he wanted Chris to like him. He wanted everyone to like him. They continued to make out. Ashton wondered if maybe, for Chris, he represented a breath of fresh air, or an adventure, or a way to reconnect with youthful idealism. He remembered what Dan had told him that night in the park.

"I think I finally figured out what sex is for!" Dan had said. "It's essentially a form of networking."

"Oh my god yes," Ashton had replied, drunkenly holding up a bottle of the fun craft beer, with a colorful label, that they had gotten from the store. "You are right! ALL sex is an exchange, all sex is transactional. That's why its necessary for a politician to USE sex – I mean look at John F. Kennedy, hahaha."

"You're so weird, Ashton," Dan had said, in his ironic, avuncular tone. "I mean I'm feeling a bit weird right now from last night – I went out with Rachel and Medea again," he noted. "But you're always like this."

His acquaintance had the archetypally handsome face of a "white American of European descent," almost like a member of the Kennedy family himself. But it was the ironic smile and manner that Ashton found most engaging, most relatable. As if he was both being sincere with the person he was talking to, and not, but also flattering the person with the impression that they were both in on the insincerity, that they both understood the lie and the reason for the lie – that they were co-conspirators.

"We are definitely gonna use sex to sell you to the Democratic constituents of Brooklyn and the Upper East Side," said Dan.

"Oh my god," repeated Ashton. "I am so excited to do this campaign."

Dan patted Ashton on the back. It was the same comforting, paternal gesture that Chris had unknowingly replicated on their walk together.

"We are so much smarter than other people," said Dan.

By "we" he of course had meant trans people. But also, maybe, possibly, he had meant just them, on that specific night, the two of them, Ashton and Dan, and no one except them. They were sitting on the bench in Prospect Park by the World War I monument. Ashton felt sentimental about the monument – it reminded him of the anime about Alexander the Great, in its depiction of masculine suffering and nobility. It was dark now, but during the day, Ashton recalled, you could see the figures – the veiled face of the Angel of Death, the soldier's expression contorted into a rictus of ecstatic pleasure/pain as he languished and was led away.

In the apartment, Ashton tried to swoon into Chris's arms (Chris was just a normal person and not trans) as if he, Ashton, were dying and Chris was the one who could lead him somewhere better, somewhere normal. They continued to make out while seated together in this fashion.

"Oh wow," Chris said after a while.

"Oh shit I'm sorry," said Ashton, jolted out of his reverie. "Sorry I am so bad at this."

"Oh no, its fine," Chris reassured him. "You are just like... kinda forceful..."

"Oh shit I'm sorry," repeated Ashton. "I was really jamming my tongue in there. God that's so gross."

"What? No, no, its fine," said Chris. "I don't want you to feel like you're doing something you don't like."

"What? No, I definitely like this," said Ashton.

He started making out with Chris less forcefully, only slightly touching his teeth and not jamming his tongue into his mouth. It wasn't that Ashton wasn't attracted to Chris. It was that the attraction that he felt was almost, in a way, antithetical to the sexual feeling. It was as if maybe the "neural pathways" that normally got "activated" during the sex act were being used for something else. Or, as if the idea and hope of what he was supposed to be feeling overshadowed whatever "real" experience he, or they, were actually having. And yet everything depended on Ashton being attracted to his date in the correct way – his friendships, his future, the personal and professional life he was trying to build for himself.

Ashton disengaged from the embrace. It was always a reliable means of initiating desire, feeling the genitals of the man. Chis had been saying all this stuff on their walk, about how a person's looks didn't matter, gender didn't matter, about how there were so many different ways for people to be sexually attractive. At the time, Ashton had argued with Chris's statements, which had seemed to him like empty virtue signaling.

"If you are not spending your life trying to be a hot dude, emulating some 'fake' ideal, what are you supposed to be doing with yourself? Like, what else is there in life?" Ashton had said. He had been joking, but also serious. It wasn't "a bit."

Yet now, as Ashton removed his sexual partner's baggy jeans and boxers in one swift motion, perfected over the course of many previous (unlike this one) only semi-politically-motivated online dates, he felt less sure of himself. What was missing? He had done everything right, dieted, wore flattering pants, yet he still could not engage with other people, sexually or emotionally.

Ashton beheld his date's engorged genitals. He now considered the masculine aesthetic – the so-called "fake ideal" – he had spent his life trying to emulate. It certainly had little in common with the cartoonish, butch gestures he had seen other trans guys making sometimes – wearing big boots, or driving a truck or whatever (it was true, as far as Ashton knew, that Dan had also once owned and driven a large truck, but that was different – Dan had been aware of the irony of owning such a vehicle, and had made fun of typical trans guys).

No, thought Ashton. Real masculinity came from being powerful and uncaring. It was the peace of mind that came from knowing you were the most important person in your own life – the main character in a coming-of-age story that involved sympathetic girlfriends, coaches, and parents, people whose main function in life it was to support you and ensure you discovered the spark of manhood in yourself that would cause you to become a genius. Ashton had, in fact, spent his life trying to be someone who had had that level of unconscious privilege. Yet now that he had superficially achieved that goal, no one seemed to have noticed. No one, or almost no one, seemed to know what it was he had superficially achieved.

"You like what you see?" said Chris again, interrupting his thoughts.

"What?"

"Haha, I'm joking."

It was just a regular dick Ashton was holding. It was not at all symbolic. Ashton did not know if he felt bad or good about this discovery. He shoved it into the back of his throat, relying on his habitual tropes of stoic masculine suffering and repression. Chris put his hand on the back of Ashton's head. Chris indicated verbally and using body language that he approved of Ashton's actions.

What was Ashton's plan for the Democratic primary for the 2018 US House elections? Dan had explained the situation to him this way: Carolyn Maloney was ready for a well-earned retirement, after serving in the House for twenty-six years, during which time she had vastly expanded Medicare coverage for women, secured billions in federal funding to help build the city's infrastructure, and was recognized by her community multiple times for introducing more resolutions, bills, and amendments to the floor than any other representative in the state. The Democratic Party wanted to replace her with Jonathan Bing, a former state assembly member for District 73, who, according to Dan, was best known in his nine years in office for co-sponsoring one of the bills that eventually helped lift the state's ban on MMA tournaments. The other person who had declared his candidacy was a younger dude, Adrian Rubinsky, an openly gay, monogamous "start-up entrepreneur" who presented himself as an alternative to inefficient, conventional politicians.

Dan had felt that Jonathan Bing was an uncharismatic candidate and that, even if he were elected, he would not fight for the needs of the district, especially its most marginalized people, with anywhere near the same energy or dedication as his predecessor. He was also dismissive of Adrian Rubinsky, with his feel-good monogamous gay identity and his centrist platform, which emphasized creating jobs, getting rid of loopholes in the federal tax code, promoting LGBTQ-inclusive sex education, and organizing after-school programs encouraging students from a wide variety of back-grounds to learn to code.

Ashton had pretended to disagree with Dan's assessments, or to have some other, nuanced opinion about the election. In reality, the contempt with which Dan talked about the other candidates drew him in and inspired in him a strange and visceral excitement. It was part of his whole thing as a man, Dan's, to always seem calm and interested, nerdy and impartial, to be always talking in a benign, amused, professorial tone about different groups and organizations that he was part of or had to deal with. But sometimes the mask would slip, it felt like, and his manner would suggest something else: a kind of cold, unlimited anger towards the world, impossible to ever satisfy or even address. It was at these moments that he was most compelling to Ashton, and that he wished this person could or would somehow become his friend.

"You know, as men, we can't sit by and watch our community get exploited by this goofy opportunist. I mean, that is what he is," Dan had said.

They were looking at the street from his open third-story window. It was surprisingly bright outside, and they were both wearing sunglasses.

"Sure, definitely. This start-up politician seems like a real douchebag!" Ashton had replied.

"If this fag is elected to Congress – which he won't be – I'll be gobsmacked if he won't try to, say, defund the MTA, or... vote for legislation limiting the money we can give to Medicaid. And the Democrats are trying to run some guy who is like sixty years old, who no one cares about, who's gonna to lose the election, who's gonna turn the district over to the Republicans!"

"Do you really think that will happen?" said Ashton.

"None of these people care about us," said Dan. "Our community – which contains, by its very nature, some of the most insightful, caring, interesting people in the world – is screwed. Unless we, you and I, act specifically to change that."

He did not pause or look at him.

"This is kind of our moment, Ashton," he asserted.

The cold anger beneath the surface of these words moved Ashton.

"Well, if you want someone to run in the primary, I'm your man!" he exclaimed. "A man with no proper sense of himself – a man with nothing inside, who could therefore be all things to all people. Ahahahaha." He was moved to laughter by his own eloquence, by what he felt to be the truth and transformative power of what he was saying, to the one person who could get it.

On the futon, Chris was putting his dick into Ashton's mouth.

"Ashton, this feels really good," said Chris.

"Oh thanks," said Ashton, briefly interrupting and then resuming his sexual activity. He felt his partner's pelvic bones. He surrendered to self-pity.

Suddenly, something brushed against his foot. A large, long-haired cat with orange-and-white fur had walked into the room and was now walking around on the floor of the "office."

"Oh, its my boyfriend's cat, sorry," said Chris.

"Oh, that's okay," said Ashton.

The cat's presence made Ashton self-conscious (as if he hadn't already been self-conscious), but it also reminded him why he was there: the boyfriend and the connection to the Working Families Party. Ashton figured that, if he successfully engaged in sex now, he would be able to ask Chris about it later. Then he would either talk to Chris's boyfriend directly, or he would ask Chris to ask the boyfriend to put him in touch with Charles Monaco, the Working Families Party's New York digital director. And this man was someone who, even if Ashton couldn't ask for a direct endorsement from the party (not yet), would be able to, in turn, introduce him to key influencers and give him actual, professional advice as to how to run a successful grassroots campaign.

That was what Ashton had told Dan he would do, and that was what he was still planning to do. Ashton turned his attention back to the oral sex he was having with Chris. It was not necessarily a bad plan.

"Sorry, uh, its kind of weird with this cat," said Ashton.

"Aw, let's get her out of here," said Chris.

Ashton watched Chris get up from the futon. The sides of his legs were pale but naturally muscular as he tried to pick up and guide the uncooperative pet. Ashton thought that, from this angle, Chris looked attractive.

"Come on, move it," said Chris.

"Don't you ever feel angry?" said Ashton. "Like when you said you didn't 'fit in' at school for being gay or whatever. Because it made you feel you were maybe better than other people?"

"Oh, I'm *so* much better than other people," said Chris. He was back on the futon. The cat was gone.

"Yeah?" said Ashton, grabbing his leg.

Chris rolled his eyes. "I was making fun of you. Come on."

Chris pulled Ashton towards him. They began to make out again. Ashton felt the outlines of his ribs, his teeth. He found himself sitting on his lap. He remembered that they were both approximately the same height. It could actually feel surprisingly natural sometimes, and not unpleasant, to be aware of the body of another person.

"I like it when you make fun of me," confessed Ashton.

"Do you want me to fuck you now?" said Chris.

"Yeah, for sure," said Ashton. "Wait."

He looked at him. He tried to think of an innocuous way to say it, something that didn't sound like it came from a trite, pedantic social media post.

"Would you want to try to, like... reciprocate the act? I mean the oral sex act. On my genitals."

"Oh," said Chris. His eyes widened. "Uh, I would feel really nervous about doing that."

"Oh yeah for sure I get it," said Ashton quickly.

"Like its a pragmatic thing. I wouldn't know what to do."

"Yeah totally," interrupted Ashton. "I agree we should fuck instead."

⁊

Even though Dan had said, "We are definitely gonna use sex," most of his campaign ideas had been much more mundane than that. For example, he had wanted Ashton to attend a meeting of the Stonewall Democratic Club of NYC. He had also wanted Ashton and "the team" to go out together to practice asking for signatures. Ashton would need to collect at least 1,250 signatures from registered Democrats in the district in order to get on the ballot for the primary in June of next year. The petitioning period hadn't started yet, but Dan had wanted them to "get used to the feeling of selling themselves in a public space," of asking strangers with little to no interest in them or their struggles for their time and attention.

"That's all politics really is," he had said. "its actually how you build a community, out of nothing."

As part of this initiative Ashton had gone to Union Square with Rachel last Saturday. Like Ashton, Rachel worked at a tech company. She was also trans. They had a brief conversation about those subjects.

"How is working at a tech company?" asked Ashton.

"It's great. I've always loved the work."

"Good," said Ashton. "It's fine for me as well. I mean, its a bit boring, but what can you do," he added, attempting to give the remark a tone of irony.

"Sure," said Rachel. "I guess coding can be a bit repetitive and frustrating."

Ashton couldn't tell if she was being sarcastic, or if she was nervous and couldn't tell that *he* was the one who was actually being sarcastic, as a kind of commentary on the inherent difficulty of all conversation. Even after all these years, he preferred to talk to people as a group, tell them stories about himself, rather than confront individuals directly. On some level, he could not offer much, individually, to most people. Still, as they walked towards the farmers' market, Ashton began to feel less awkward about being in Rachel's proximity. He took off his jacket. It was an unusually warm day. Ashton thought maybe he looked pretty good, even while holding a clipboard. He thought maybe they both looked pretty good. They were part of the fabric of urban life, modern and engaged.

"It's too bad he didn't want to go out petitioning with us," said Ashton.

"You mean Dan?" asked Rachel.

"Who else?" said Ashton. "I mean, he is the only other guy working on this campaign. Like, besides me."

"Yes, well," said Rachel, as if Ashton had intentionally said something provocative. "I mean, he already has a lot of experience with this stuff."

"Haha, is that true? I just can't imagine him asking strangers to sign stuff. Or, like – 'selling himself in a public space.'"

Ashton laughed again. Actually, he had never seen Dan during the day at all, except for that one time in his apartment (when he'd said that it was their moment, and they'd both looked out the window). This reclusiveness was another one of Dan's poignant vulnerabilities...

"Strangers?" said Rachel suddenly. "These are your future constituents, my dude!"

All at once, she was loud and boisterous, slapping Ashton on the back. The trans women who were Dan's friends sometimes acted ironically masculine like this.

"Haha, how true," said Ashton.

"Anyway, he's really good at this stuff," said Rachel. "He's a smart guy. He did a lot for me when we worked on Congresswoman Maloney's 2014 campaign."

Ashton had already heard all this. Rachel was always talking about how important working part-time for Carolyn Maloney's 2014 congressional campaign had been for her, what a turning point it had been in her life. That was where she had met Dan, and that was when he had convinced her to transition, leave behind her previous office job (with its poor trans healthcare benefits), and break up with her "boring cis girlfriend." Ashton often saw Rachel at Dan's apartment – she still sometimes referred to it as "our place" – and whenever he ran into her there, she would hold forth about how important her gender transition had been for her emotionally, how it had made her "stop dissociating" and "start caring about things," and the mixed, but ultimately rewarding, consequences of that change.

Ashton could not relate. He had always cared about things. That wasn't the problem. He wished Dan were here, to act as an intermediary between him and these women.

"I guess its hot that you admire him so much," said Ashton.

"Heh." Rachel smiled pointedly but said nothing more on this topic.

During the course of the next hour, Ashton and Rachel found five registered Democrats who were willing to sign their petition. As Dan had predicted, no one cared that the date written on the petition – March 18, 2018 – was eleven months from now. March 18, 2018, was the start of the official petitioning period, and, supposedly, any signatures they collected before that date would be considered invalid. Dan had figured they should go out to collect signatures anyway, and see what happened.

"It's a bureaucratic gatekeeping thing and it doesn't matter. And the people who are signing these things won't care. These are standard tactics, Ashton," he'd said, and he'd mostly been right.

Then one person, the sixth would-be signer, wouldn't give them his address. This man, a typical-looking (Ashton thought) District 12 resident holding a reusable shopping bag and wearing a baseball cap that said "The Center for Fiction," listened patiently while Ashton and Rachel explained who Ashton was, and why he was running for the Democratic House seat for District 12. They talked about Ashton's platform as a candidate: tenant protections, infrastructure repairs, Medicare expansion, ending the war on drugs. They mentioned that Ashton — the candidate — was trans, and how his experience within the LGBTQ community informed his desire to serve the district's most marginalized residents.

The man interrupted them. "Listen, I support what you're doing. I support New Yorkers helping New Yorkers. I just don't feel comfortable giving out my address."

"I understand," said Rachel. "The thing is, you kind of have to put your address down, or its not valid."

"Yeah," Ashton put in. "It's not like we're telemarketers."

He was trying to sound less brittle and more jocular than Rachel, leveraging (he hoped) his male privilege to attract more supporters.

Rachel looked at Ashton sternly. "We're definitely not telemarketers," she agreed.

"Hm," said the man.

"Would you like to give us your address?" said Rachel, her expression a bland mask of political efficiency.

The man put down his shopping bag.

"Okay," he sighed. "You've convinced me."

He elaborately searched his pockets for a pen, did not find one, and then used the pen attached to Rachel's clipboard to write his signature. He handed Rachel the attached pen. He looked at her intently, and shook her hand.

"I've signed your petition."

"Thank you," said Rachel.

"You have my support. You really do," said the man emphatically. "We need all kinds of people on the ballot."

"We absolutely do," said Rachel.

She vigorously shook his hand, until the man finally let go. After he left, Ashton looked at the clipboard.

"I guess he didn't put down his address."

Rachel did not answer.

"Well, we can probably look it up," said Ashton. "Like, from the name?"

Ashton watched Rachel as she kept looking in the direction of the man's departure. He saw the city's residents energetically engaging in commerce, lining up in front of food stands and farmers' market tents, talking to each other in groups.

"Oh yeah, that man probably thought *you* were the trans candidate," Ashton felt compelled to add.

Rachel turned to him. "Why would he think that?"

"I guess when most people think of trans people they think of trans women. They always ignore trans guys. It's an unfortunate combination of how people are sexist towards women and sexist towards men."

"I don't think that was what was going on," she said coldly.

Rachel walked a few steps and put her shoulder bag down on the concrete park barrier. Ashton followed her.

"I'm used to it," said Ashton. "It does suck."

Rachel put her clipboard inside the bag. She took out a pair of sunglasses from the bag and put them on. Their lime-green frames matched her top.

"Listen, my dude," said Rachel. "I'm feeling kind of tired."

"Oh yeah, I get it," said Ashton.

"I think I might be done for the day," said Rachel.

Before Ashton could say anything else, she picked up her shoulder bag and started to walk towards the train.

"Wait," Ashton shouted.

But she did not turn around. She was gone.

Ashton looked around. A group of people were eating hot dogs. Another group of people were gathered around a large Bernese mountain dog, petting and gesturing at the dog (he knew the type of dog it was, because he had looked up dog breeds when he had first started talking to Chris about his family). No one noticed that Ashton had been yelling at his canvassing partner. He tried to think of the people as his future constituents, and not strangers. He resumed his task.

In the next hour, working alone, Ashton was able to collect three additional signatures. He went to a nearby library to prepare for his speech.

Later that same day, at the meeting of the Stonewall Democratic Club, Ashton felt anxious about what had happened at the farmers' market, but was able to channel his anxieties into a speech that he gave to the whole club, where he touched on topics such as campaign finance reform, inefficiencies in the city's public housing program, and the need for more accessible healthcare for trans and gender non-conforming individuals. Just when he thought for sure Dan was not going to show up, he was there. He had come with Rachel. She seemed happy about the speech. They both seemed happy.

Free of his usual inhibitions after the excitement of the speech, Ashton embraced Dan.

"That was a great speech. I loved your speech," said Dan.

"Thank you," said Ashton.

5

Ashton felt the hand on the back of his head, the other hand pushing him into the futon. As he had sex with Chris, he thought about Dan. He looked at the hardwood floor, with its slight, underwhelming irregularities. His self-pity reached a kind of crescendo. He had deliberately positioned himself as Dan's instrument. He wanted Dan to use him. He felt seen by Dan. He wanted Dan to see him now.

Ashton focused on a space on the floor where the gaps in the wood converged. What would they even do together? Maybe Dan would force Ashton to perform oral sex on him – and his genitals would turn out to be just as upsetting as anyone else's genitals, if not more, and that would be meaningful for both of them. Or maybe he would just smirk at Ashton, in his paternal, avuncular way – and that, too, would have sexual and emotional meaning.

Really, Ashton had not thought it through that far. He really was "a person with nothing inside," just like he'd told Dan, but not in a way that was necessarily bad. Even though Ashton feared and slightly loathed most people, he also had a high capacity for admiring others. And he knew Dan was similar to him in that way. He did not need to have sex with him – or go to his apartment – to be totally certain of that fact.

At the height of this feeling of self-pity and tragic certainty, Ashton heard the door open. A bespectacled, bearded man in a bathrobe peered into the room. He saw Ashton. Chris stopped his pelvic thrusting.

"Oh, sorry," said the bearded, rumpled person. He spoke in a creaking, low-pitched voice. He did not close the door. Lying on top of Ashton, Chris moved his body slightly.

"Shouldn't you be in bed?" asked Chris.

"Yeah," said the person.

Ashton knew this was the boyfriend – the one who maintained the servers for the Working Families Party. He had been in the apartment this whole time. The boyfriend slowly shifted his weight from side to side.

"Sorry, I was just looking for Sandy Cheeks," said the boyfriend, coughing.

"Oh my god," said Chris, jerking his body to one side in mock frustration. "She's not in here. Why don't you check in the kitchen?"

"I already checked in the kitchen," said the boyfriend. He coughed again, covering his mouth with the sleeve of his bathrobe.

"She probably got stuck behind the washing machine," said Chris. "Sandy Cheeks is the cat," he explained to Ashton. "He's always bothering her," he added, indicating the boyfriend.

Ashton turned his head. He watched as the boyfriend proceeded to search the entire "office" for the cat, looking behind the futon, between the collapsible shelves, and under the desk with the two monitors. As Chris had predicted, he failed to find the cat. He finally gave up, coughed into a tissue, and left. Ashton tried to wave at him, but he was gone.

"Sorry about that," said Chris.

"Oh yeah, no problem. It's cool that you guys have a washing machine," said Ashton.

"Haha. They put it in the kitchen for some reason? But yeah, its great."

The boyfriend had not closed the door all the way, and Chris got up to close it after him. Then he maneuvered towards the desk, one hand covering his midsection.

"I'm gonna play some music now," he said.

When Chris turned on the computer, Ashton saw that the desktop background on both monitors was a picture of Chris standing next to the boyfriend in front of a suburban house, alongside Chris's parents (Ashton could tell who they were) and three dogs. The dogs looked like generic retriever mixes. They did not appear to be any specific breed.

Chris opened the music player program. Ashton heard the whimsical synths that marked the start of the song "Kids" by MGMT.

Chris sat down heavily on the futon. "Oh man," he said. "I'm sorry. We're gonna have to finish kind of quickly here."

"That's cool," said Ashton.

"Cool," said Chris.

He leaned back on the futon. Making sure, swift, rhythmic movements, he began to manually stimulate his, at first, only semi-erect genitals. He made rapid progress. After approximately 30 seconds, Chris reached towards Ashton with his other hand. Ashton thought about the logistics of what Chris was proposing.

"Uh, no, I'm like all good," said Ashton.

"Are you sure?" asked Chris.

"Yeah, definitely."

Chris briefly looked concerned, but soon resumed his activity. He closed his eyes and made, again, rapid progress. He finished with at least two minutes left before the end of "Kids," sighing and resting his head on the back of the futon.

After some thought, Ashton put his arm under and around Chris's neck. They both sat like this, fully nude, through two additional songs from whatever playlist Chris had on – "My Name Is Jonas" by Weezer and "The Middle" by Jimmy Eat World.

"I'm getting kind of cold," said Chris finally. "You sure you're, uh, all good?"

"I'm totally fine," said Ashton. "Thank you."

"Cool," said Chris. "Well, you don't need to thank me," he added.

He began to put on his underwear.

"Love You Madly" by Cake started playing from the speakers mounted above the desk. Ashton listened to the jaunty, insinuating singing.

"I guess we'd better wrap this up," said Chris, now wearing, again, the same baggy T-shirt and jeans Ashton had helped him remove earlier. "My boyfriend's been sick all week."

"Oh yeah, I know how that is," said Ashton.

He started to put on his own clothes. He had never had a boyfriend or long-term romantic partner before. He paused.

"Oh hey," he began, trying to sound casual. "Speaking of which, is your boyfriend still doing that stuff for the Working Families Party? Like, the servers and stuff?"

Chris waited by the door for Ashton.

"What? I think so?"

"Cool," said Ashton.

"Yeah, he goes over there maybe once a month. He's pretty busy with his day job though..."

"I definitely know how that is," said Ashton. "I definitely get being busy."

Ashton finished putting on his boxers. He had gotten them in a size Small, in a fine check pattern, to emphasize his relatively small hips, achieved through years of (post-testosterone) meal portioning and jogging. He put on his black pants and tight button-down shirt. He laced up his large boots, which had nothing to do with his masculinity or desire to emulate masculinity.

Chris walked Ashton to the door of the apartment. On the way, they passed through the kitchen, where he showed Ashton the washing machine, remarking, again, on its inconvenient location. They did not see the boyfriend or cat on the way out.

During the train ride home, Ashton wondered if it would make sense to try to go on a second date with Chris. He had not gotten in touch with Charles Monaco, the Working Families Party, or the boyfriend. For a moment, Ashton wondered if his thoughts had any reality outside of himself, if there would ever even be an election, a primary, an endorsement. But he was not in his early twenties anymore. It was not useful to think in those terms. It was just as Dan had said. The key was to keep going to events, keep messaging people, keep building a presence in the community. If he didn't message Chris, Chris wouldn't message him back. If he didn't message Dan, Dan wouldn't message him back. It was obvious. Ashton wondered if, as the US congressional representative of the 12th district, he would still feel as alone.

SIGNS

"I'm locking up the classroom," said Ms. Binding, the eighth-grade English teacher. "You can't stay here."

"I know, I know," said Complicity, cringing, apologetic.

"Much as I would love that," added the teacher.

Complicity repositioned the papers and pencils on her desk. She was the only one left in the room, and she didn't want to leave. Something was unresolved.

She pushed forward the copy of the book she was reading. She wanted the teacher to be able to glimpse the title: the words *Death Comes for the Archbishop* situated across the top in a pleasing, conservative sans serif typeface.

Complicity had latched onto Willa Cather's 1927 historical novel – a fictionalized biography of a missionary priest during the early days of America's celebrated westward expansion – because of its understated depiction of a homosocial relationship between two members of the Catholic clergy in an isolating, austere physical and social environment. The book had a tone of melancholy inevitability – a sense of the doomed and unrealized nature of all relationships, mediated as they were by oppressive social and political norms – and it culminated in the main character's titular death.

Complicity was hoping the teacher would notice the book's title and, perhaps, say something. But that was not happening. Ms. Binding merely stood there, waiting, inches from her desk. Complicity imagined hearing the airy rustle of the teacher's long skirt (or skirtlike pants). Her alienating feminine energy seemed to radiate down onto Complicity's seated form. There was something disappointing, Complicity reflected, about women teachers, books written by women. But still, it was better than nothing. And Complicity longed for it, whatever that thing was that the books and teachers (even if they were women) promised or implied.

"I am about to leave," said Complicity, but her voice sounded stilted.

She had received detailed, positive comments from Ms. Binding about her last assignment – a short story about the 1966 University of Texas mass shooting, written from the point of view of the mass shooter. Maybe it was the memory of that praise that was making Complicity feel as though she could linger in the room.

She tried again. "Sorry, its just that this book was so interesting, I didn't even hear the bell ring."

"Hmm," said Ms. Binding, "What's it about?"

"Oh, nothing," said Complicity quickly.

She didn't know how to start talking about it, or what she expected out of the conversation. She probably needed to show some resistance, as if the teacher got the information out of her unwillingly. Or maybe it simply wasn't the right time? Complicity gathered the heap of out-of-date assignments and photocopied sheets on her desk. She pushed them into her backpack and started to walk away.

"Okay, bye," said Complicity.

"Haha," said the teacher. "I'll see you tomorrow."

Complicity took a few more steps, then stopped. She was taken aback by the discomfort of having directly addressed another person by saying "bye." The teacher's disruptive, feminine appearance and presentation as she watched Complicity – long hair pinned back; flowing, maternal clothing – did not help. She continued to stand in the doorway without moving.

"Well, actually, why don't you walk me to my car," said Ms. Binding finally.

"Oh, okay," said Complicity, trying to show the proper amount of surprise.

She put the book in her backpack and followed the teacher outside. They walked together in the shade of the portable structures. Complicity crossed her arms as she walked. There were no mirrors or reflective surfaces around in which she could look at herself (examples: windows, spherical mirrors meant to prevent blind spots in offices and hallways).

"Phew, its really bright out here," said Ms. Binding.

"For sure," said Complicity.

She squinted at the light reflecting off the blacktop and, past it, the distant walls of the school campus. She could hear and see her fellow students playing nearby, their voices indecipherable and, perhaps, slightly hostile.

"They could have planted some trees," said Ms. Binding, gesturing to the asphalt around them.

"Yeah definitely," said Complicity. "I like trees."

Complicity thought about what she should say. The story about the UT mass shooting had been based on a movie she had seen while watching TV after school (typically the emotional highlight of her day). It had been meant to shock the perceived sensibilities of school and teacher – and yet the teacher had responded with praise. Ms. Binding had commended Complicity's, in her words, "high level of research" into the historic events of the story, as well as her evocation of the unnamed narrator's "voice." She stated that she had enjoyed Complicity's depiction of the young man's sadness – manifesting in the story as pity and disdain, a refusal to see the humanity of his fellow beings. Complicity wondered what she would say if the teacher asked where she got the idea for the story. She would refute any implication that she identified with the main character. She would say that it was the purpose of art to show life – to show reality – from a different point of view.

"So, uh, the book I was reading," said Complicity – she was going to start by talking about the book – "it was called *Death Comes for the Archbishop*. I actually didn't like it that much. I thought it was bad."

"Really – I thought it was good," said Ms. Binding.

"Oh, so you've read it?"

"Yes."

Complicity wondered what to say next. Even though she was the one who had brought it up, she was not sure how she felt about the English teacher – with her medium-length blond hair, her moralizing, feminine speech style, her lack of popularity (probably) among the students, her sentimental love (apparently) of trees – actually liking the book. What would it mean for the story of Archbishop Father Jean-Marie Latour and his lifetime of service to an impossible ideal if the teacher had perceived its value?

They kept walking. The parking lot was coming into view, an expanse of concrete behind a double row of cement blocks.

"Well, anyway, I thought the book was bad, because, hm – well, it asked you to identify too much with the main character," said Complicity.

But Ms. Binding paused. "I've actually been wanting to talk to you about something else."

"Huh? Like what?"

"You really don't know what it is?"

In reality, Complicity did know. In fact, it was probably this, and not, after all, a conversation about the book, that was going to precipitate the emotional catharsis she had been seeking after the whole time.

Ms. Binding sighed. "You can be a talented writer," she began.

This was what Complicity wanted to hear. "Oh, I don't think so..." she said.

"Is this some sort of false modesty you're exhibiting?"

"What? No way."

"You are about to fail my class," said Ms. Binding.

"Oh," said Complicity.

Complicity had not forgotten about the issue of grades, but she had subsumed it into her general contemplation of, first, the UT mass shooter (a former child prodigy and abuse victim), second, the priest and his doomed Catholicism (his final entombment in the cathedral he built after a lifetime in the desert) and, now, her own presumed writing talent. But she was going to have to let the teacher drag out the whole shameful affair.

"I just thought— " said Complicity.

She did not need to finish telling the teacher what she thought. Complicity had submitted some, but not all, of the major assignments for the class, and had not submitted any of the assigned homework, which put her firmly in the category of failing to meet the school's most basic criteria of scholarly productivity.

They arrived at the teacher's car. Ms. Binding began, again, to speak more abstractly about Complicity as a person — her cognitive abilities, her latent potential as a writer and thinker.

"Oh, I don't think I'm actually that good," Complicity reiterated, "I barely spent any time on that story."

It felt good to deliberately lie to the teacher. Yet at some point in the middle of Ms. Binding's disquisition, Complicity began to exhibit the emotional vulnerability she hated. With a shameful lack of control, she began to cry. But fortunately the teacher did not notice, or pretended not to notice.

"Is there a way I can get a better grade in the class?" Complicity said finally, at the end of the embarrassing yet still emotionally cathartic episode.

"What's that?" said Ms. Binding. She yanked on her car's passenger-side door. Papers were strewn everywhere inside it, as well as what appeared to be piles of flowing clothing.

"Shit" said Ms. Binding. She looked at Complicity. "Sorry, the lock doesn't work," she explained apologetically.

Complicity gazed down. It was a white compact car. Except for the personal items within, it was unremarkable, like any other vehicle one might see in a parking lot or at an intersection. There was definitely something poignant about seeing an adult's car.

"Can I still get a better grade in the class?" repeated Complicity. "Like if I turn everything in from now on?"

The teacher pulled and shook the handle. Finally, the car door swung open. "Success," she said.

She faced Complicity, hands triumphantly on hips. Then she ducked back in through the open door. Complicity watched her rifle through the mound of fabric on the front seat of the car. Probably more of those feminine jackets and scarves. The teacher emerged holding a large book.

"And yes," said Ms. Binding, answering Complicity's question. "You can still get a B in the class. Here is what you can do."

She showed Complicity the tome. It was called *The Bakhtin Reader: the Selected Writings of Bakhtin, Medvedev, Voloshinov, by Pam Morris.*

"This is one of my favorite academic writers," said Ms. Binding. "I don't expect you to know this, but Pam Morris has actually compiled a really important book on language and novels."

"Wow, awesome."

The tome was a light lavender and fuschia color with cursive writing on the front. It looked well-worn. Except for the pink hue – due to, perhaps, it being, again, the work of a female author – it looked like a serious, college-level work.

"Yes, it is 'awesome'," said Ms. Binding. "Bakhtin's writing on the novel is awesome. And relevant. And this book is a great introduction to those ideas."

"Wow, I can't wait to read it," said Complicity.

"Well, you will have to do more than read it," said Ms. Binding. "If you want to make up for your missing homework, you can start by writing a five-paragraph essay analyzing a book that you enjoyed, utilizing the concepts in this text. Or did not enjoy," she added with a slight smile. She was talking about *Death Comes for the Archbishop*, which Complicity had claimed not to have liked.

"Wow," said Complicity for the third time. Some of the tension she had felt earlier was starting to subside. She looked in the car, scanning the dashboard for incriminating personal objects.

"I thought you personally would like this book," said Ms. Binding, indicating the pink academic text. "I thought it would interest you, because, well – given the strong use of 'voice' in your writing to explore otherwise maligned or potentially unsympathetic perspectives."

"Well, that's exciting," said Complicity. She did actually feel slightly excited. So the teacher had, in fact, found her perspective unsympathetic! She looked in the car again. She thought she saw something else on the dashboard. "A condom," thought Complicity involuntarily. She quickly looked up. "So I can really get a B if I write this essay?"

"It will count towards a B, yes."

"Wow," said Complicity for the fourth and final time. "Uh, thanks."

It was not a condom. Complicity could see that it was just a container of zero-calorie gum, purchased, intentionally no doubt, from a convenience store or vending machine, with money that the teacher earned teaching middle school English. Almost equally incriminating, in a way. But of course, realistically, any condom packages or similarly private items would be stored somewhere out of sight.

   "If you finish the essay, we can talk about what else you can do to improve your grade," said Ms. Binding. "I am asking a lot of you. But I am also making an exception for you, Complicity."

   "I understand," said Complicity. "You won't be disappointed."

5

After the conversation, Complicity ambled over to the place where she typically spent the lunch hour – a secluded gap between two school buildings, separated by a patch of dried grass. The canyon-like walls of the buildings provided shelter from the sun.

   Complicity sat on the ground, leaned back against a terracotta-colored wall, and opened the hefty volume. She decided she would actually try hard on this essay. That would show the teacher, if she actually started turning everything in. She began to read the introduction.

   "The work in this book is renowned for its innovative and dynamic perception of language," she read. "Its rejection of a structuralist view of language as a monolithic conceptual system."

   It looked as though – cover notwithstanding – the woman, Pam Morris, truly was merely the compiler or editor of this text. The majority of the writing was by a man, a historic figure, an academic. Complicity had earned, perhaps, the teacher's trust. She moved on to the first page of the first essay. She resolved to try to subvert the expectations of whatever it was this book was saying, or whatever it was that the teacher thought this book was saying that had made her decide that she liked this book. However, the book's words proved difficult to interpret.

"Everything ideological possesses meaning: It represents, depicts, or stands for something lying outside itself. Without signs there is no ideology," said the essay. "A physical object equals itself... it does not signify anything but wholly co-incides with its particular, given nature." This language continued for several paragraphs.

Complicity got up to stare at her reflection in the windows of one of the buildings. From this angle, when it was just her face, she looked almost normal. She sat back down. She tried to parse the text. It seemed to be making a distinction between signs and objects. The essay was saying that a sign was a special type of physical object – one that tried to say something or mean something. So then, Complicity wondered, were some objects "neutral," without any special meaning beyond what they "were"? What were "objects"? Complicity considered the physical space around her, the clumps of brown grass, the lumps of beige-and-brown stucco on the walls. Was an object separate from the word referring to that object? That was probably the kind of internal debate a sensitive priest would have, alone in his stark room. Or, perhaps, while gazing upon the statues of Christian saints he would find in the simple homes of the people. How could he ever have a meaningful relationship with these peasants, who lived conventional lives and were actually comforted by religion? Complicity spent so long on these thoughts that she did not have time to read the second page of the essay before lunch break ended.

The difficulty with the book and its essays continued upon Complicity's return home. After she arrived at her parents' house, she went to the TV. She was watching a music video when her younger sister entered the room. Complicity immediately lunged at her.

"You're such a piece of shit," yelled Complicity.

"I didn't do anything!"

"What the fuck," said Complicity, "why did you just come in here? Like in the room. There is something seriously wrong with this family."

Later, Complicity tried to make her sister feel better by proposing they watch *Malcolm in the Middle*, a show they both purportedly enjoyed. Yet she quickly became depressed by its depiction of a rowdy family with four teen- and preteen-age sons. Outside, the sun was starting to set.

"I hate this. Let's watch *Seventh Heaven*. It's a good Christian show." Complicity laughed maliciously.

"No!" exclaimed her sister.

Her simpering lack of enthusiasm genuinely angered Complicity. She loved hate-watching the show about the unintellectual Christian pastor, who thought religion was about enforcing traditional social norms rather than a chance to meditate on humanity's flawed state. But before Complicity could finish telling her sister this, their parents arrived. The unpleasantness of the sibling dynamic, with its steady undercurrent of shame, persisted into the hours-long process of dinner preparation and cleanup.

Afterwards, Complicity returned to the first page of the essay. "A sign is a phenomenon of the external world. Both the sign itself and all the effects it produces (all those actions, reactions and new signs it elicits in the surrounding social milieu) occur in outer experience," she read.

This statement did not seem to be correct. If this essay was about reading and words – and it probably was – then the act of perceiving, understanding, and remembering words definitely seemed like something that happened in the brain, a phenomenon of the internal world. Complicity noticed with dismay that some of the specific plot points of *Death Comes for the Archbishop*, which her whole extra credit assignment was supposed to be about, were already becoming hard to remember. Would Father Latour be disappointed by her lack of rigor? But no. She recalled the climax, as far as she was concerned, of the whole book. The Archbishop had summoned his friend Father Joseph back to the diocese, even though there had been no ecclesiastical reason to do so. He had spent three days contemplating their friendship and what it meant. He had named, referenced, and acknowledged, in the privacy of his mind, that special feeling of – longing, perhaps? maybe even a very problematic and questionable sort of hope? – that informed the whole narrative.

And then Father Joseph was writing another letter, and he became aware of it too. The novel switched to his point of view and he began to reflect on the Archbishop's "exceptional qualities", the "differences in their natures". It was that feeling of mutual, chaste admiration that informed the Catholic missionary work they did, even though (as neither of them would admit) the actual value of that work was questionable or maybe sort of harmful. And then, as Father Joseph was writing, a single teardrop fell on the letter – and the Archbishop saw it fall!

Complicity looked for the quote: "The Bishop saw a drop of water splash down upon the violet script and spread. He turned quickly and went out through the arched doorway."

Complicity closed the pink textbook and did not reopen it at any point in the subsequent month. She also did not submit any more English homework that month. The few fiction books that Complicity read during that time failed to make the same impression as Willa Cather's 1927 novel, perhaps because she had already begun to mythologize her own experience of the latter work. The night before the five-paragraph essay was due, she decided to reread as much of *Death Comes for the Archbishop* as she could. Then she started to write the essay.

"Willa Cather's 1927 novel *Death Comes for the Archbishop* is full of signs," she wrote. She looked at *The Bakhtin Reader*. She replaced the word "signs" with "what the writers Mikhail Bakhtin and Pam Morris called 'signs.'" She thought about what she should do. "I think signs are phenomena of the internal world and not the external world," she continued. But she was unable to add a third sentence.

After a fitful sleep at her desk, Complicity went to school with a feeling of dread, which intensified during the walk to Ms. Binding's classroom. However, as she approached the classroom, when she saw the door at the end of its familiar ramp, when she saw and smelled the plastic chairs and blue carpeting within, she felt something – a sense of reprieve.

Something was blocking the harsh light that had been bearing down on her the whole day, physically and mentally. She stood under the awning of the building. "It's like a sign of the cross in the desert," thought Complicity. "An internal sign," she clarified to herself. She turned around, and did not enter the classroom.

As her peers filed into their respective rooms, Complicity continued to walk past the rows of portable structures. She saw the empty blacktop with basketball hoops to one side. She saw the parking lot ahead, with its modest cluster of cars. The sky was mercifully blank as she crossed over the double barrier of cement blocks. The teacher's white car was still parked in the same spot. Complicity approached the vehicle. As she walked, she glimpsed her distorted reflection in the windows of the other cars. If she had her arms crossed, in profile, she really did look casual and maybe even a bit athletic — like a teen in the Target catalog that lay on the kitchen table of her home. The squashed-looking image was not ideal, but still legible.

Complicity put her face up against the window of the white car. As before, its interior appeared strewn with papers and books. Mounds of clothing covered much of the back seat. Women's clothes. A few books lay on the dashboard. Complicity read the familiar titles: *Shabanu: Daughter of the Wind*; *A Yellow Raft in Blue Water*. Copies of the assigned reading — disappointing women's books written by women. The rectangular object that Complicity had once, briefly, imagined to be a package of condoms was gone.

Complicity paused. The parking lot was empty. She could hear sparse traffic in the street beyond. After a moment,

Complicity pulled on the passenger-side door handle. It did not open. She began to shake the handle in the same way that she had seen the teacher do earlier. She recalled how upset she had felt then, listening to her criticisms. Now, she was not vulnerable to that feeling. Slowly, the lock moved into the unlocked position. The door swung open, and Complicity got inside. She had just broken into the teacher's car.

Once she was comfortably situated on the front seat, Complicity adjusted herself to her new surroundings. She was now looking out of, instead of into, the unfamiliar vehicle. In front of her, she saw the street, with its vista of intermittent driveways and trees, and, beyond – though she could not see it, but she knew it was there – a distant gas station, a place one could drive to and, perhaps, purchase a frozen drink or Popsicle (or, if one were a woman concerned about her broad figure, zero-calorie gum). Behind her, she saw the back of the car, with its scandalous trove of womanly garments and, probably, even worse artifacts. Complicity grabbed a stack of papers from the floor. Once again, she had the feeling of being in that liminal space where the reality of objects, as opposed to their verbal definition, was unclear or up for debate.

"Maybe its like I'm doing that essay after all," thought Complicity. "Or, at least, its kind of like I'm doing research for that essay."

The stack of papers turned out to be homework, weeks' worth of assignments that Complicity hadn't done. She took a moment to feel angry at the other students' hideous drawings, the smug ugliness of their work, the round letter shapes on the girls' handwriting. Then she turned her attention to the back seat. What was back there? Complicity reached over and, after a moment's hesitation, stuck her whole hand into the fabrics heaped atop its vinyl surface.

The pile was shallower than she expected. Complicity grabbed what felt like a large piece of clothing and held up – a T-shirt? It was a normal, black color. Complicity herself owned many such shirts. The T-shirt said "Oracle". She recognized it as the logo of a company that made database software.

Complicity rifled through the pile of clothes. She needed to know more about its contents. Maybe she would find a sports bra? If the teacher was worried about her weight, it was likely that she would practice aerobics or a similar activity that required athletic intimate wear, which she might have left behind on the back seat. Yet even after a thorough search, the only clothing Complicity could find were more T-shirts.

Complicity climbed into the back of the car. She began to search everywhere – underneath the seats, behind the seat cushions. She found a button that enabled her to fold down the back seat. Complicity pressed down and gazed into the trunk of the car. She felt as if she was on the brink of a vital discovery.

Then Complicity figured out what it was. She realized that the T-shirts, which she had crumpled into a corner during the course of her detailed inspection, didn't belong to the teacher at all. That would explain their masculine cut and color, the presence of a database company logo. They belonged to a man. The teacher was physically, sexually involved with this man. After they completed their sex acts, their clothing would mingle and indiscriminately show up in the private spaces of either party — such as a car. Ms. Binding always made a point of saying her name was "Miz" Binding in a way that did not reflect on her marital status. Complicity had nothing but contempt for the practice. She held up one of the man's T-shirts to her face and inhaled its slightly floral scent.

Complicity decided to stay in the car for the entire lunch period. After lunch period was over, she continued to hide in the car. In the middle of sixth period, Ms. Binding returned to find Complicity stretched out in the back seat, her face covered in one of the teacher's recently washed shirts. She had done laundry earlier. During the interaction that followed, Complicity recalled Father Joseph's last assessment of his lifelong friend:

"Doubtless Bishop Latour's successors would be men of a different fiber. But God had His reasons... Perhaps it pleased Him to grace the beginning of a new era and a vast new diocese by a fine personality. And perhaps, after all, something would remain through the years to come: some ideal, or memory, or legend."

THE MOST DANGEROUS GAME

When I was fourteen I got into Magic: The Gathering. I only had one friend from the ages of twelve to sixteen and we played Magic: The Gathering together. Although Ilya wasn't really a friend I "chose" for myself, our parents were friends and we were forced together due to having "no other friends", i.e. at school, as I mentioned previously. But despite his shortcomings, Ilya was an adequate friend. I liked having a "friend's house" to go to on the weekends, riding a lime-green mountain bike that said *Huffy* on the side in huge letters, such as I had seen my betters riding several years prior, in sixth grade. Ilya's parents seemed nice, unlike mine, and I liked to think that they thought we were romantically involved, which we definitely were not. I liked to think that they thought I was "good for" their son, that they thought I was better than him – which I definitely was. At Magic.

Magic: The Gathering is a collectible card game with attractive, fantasy-themed cards and a complex, evolving framework of rules. You try to put together a powerful deck out of the hundreds of different cards, and then you play against other people's decks.

"So to be good at this game, you have to buy more cards?" said my mom, when I tried to explain it to her. "She has to buy more cards to be good at this game," she repeated to my dad.

My dad didn't answer and went outside.

"Shut up!" I couldn't resist interjecting. "I wish I hadn't said anything about Magic!"

As I said this, I watched my dad stand outside with a cigarette. I felt embarrassed for him that he had a daughter as his only child. It must have been so emasculating for him.

My mom often criticized me for my grades and appearance at this time. She also berated me for spending so much time with someone like Ilya, who was not an asset to me socially or intellectually. In the back of my mind, I thought she was probably right. I was just a passive person, she said, like my father. I thought she was probably right about that too. To feel better about this, I started trying to reinvent myself as someone who was good at Magic.

I went on the internet to read about deck building strategies. I read a lot of forum posts and got excited about Magic: The Gathering-related news, such as the release of a new expansion, an upcoming tournament, or a minor change in the rules. I decided that the type of deck I needed to use was the "control" deck. Instead of attacking the opponent directly, it relied on cards that limited the options available to each player. This seemed extremely romantic to me, to win by exerting passive control of a situation.

This whole time, I did not play against anyone other than Ilya. He was somewhat lacking in imagination and, at times, annoying – always liking the obvious, powerful cards –

but we shared a mutual love of trivia and rules, and spent many fulfilling hours sitting on the floor of his room, going through the illustrated cards one by one. I enjoyed the art on the cards almost as much as I enjoyed contemplating each card's role in the overall rules framework. The cards' depictions of fantasy landscapes, pseudo-medieval people, and otherworldly beings looked both enticing and approachable. It looked like something I could replicate.

Ilya's Magic strategy consisted of stealing rares from his ten-year-old cousin, who was the only person he ever played with besides me. Soon, I started to beat him easily with my Control deck. His parents didn't seem to mind that he spent all day in his room playing video games, rather than improving himself; maybe that was why he was not as motivated as I was to get good at Magic. For my part, I developed an elaborate fantasy of myself as a tournament-level player, even though I still never joined any tournaments or played against anyone besides Ilya. Ilya thought I tried too hard and was scared of my mom.

🍂

Then, during my senior year of high school, my life underwent a disruption. I joined an online fantasy art gallery, and started to put up a lot of carefully shaded Magic: The Gathering-inspired art. I was sitting in an empty classroom, finishing a pencil drawing inspired by the "Marhault Elsdragon" Magic card that I kept prominently displayed at the front of my binder, even though it was not really a good card, and not part of my deck. The card's flavor text said:

"Marhault Elsdragon follows a strict philosophy, never letting emotions cloud his thoughts. No chance observer could imagine the rage in his heart."

As I was putting the finishing touches on the drawing, trying to correctly render the elven general's strict, morose expression, a girl from my school, who I knew was in theater but who was not popular otherwise, deigned to address me.

"You," she said.

I looked up from my desk, dazed. She acted as if we had spoken to each other before.

"You're in my World History class," she said, by way of explanation.

Yes, I had seen her in the class. She often argued with the teacher, complaining about how historic figures didn't always conform to her exact standards of moral conduct (informed, no doubt, by sentimental modern musicals and plays). This was the one non-AP class I was taking, I reflected grimly.

"You have the most amazing facial expressions in class," she said. "You're just like – not even remotely present."

She put a careless hand on my shoulder.

"Do you have autism?" she asked. "My boyfriend was saying you might have undiagnosed autism."

"No?" I said.

The girl leaned over to look more closely at what I was drawing.

"That's a pretty good picture," she said. She pointed at the figure. "That actually kind of looks like my boyfriend."

I tried to think of who her boyfriend might be. I didn't think someone like her would have a boyfriend.

"It's for my college application," I said finally.

That night, I dreamt that the theater girl approached me sexually. She was very forward in the dream, taking her clothes off in the empty classroom and begging me to have sex with her right on the floor. I was shocked if not entirely surprised by this lurid turn of events; yet I was reasonable in my rejection. I said I wasn't a lesbian, but would be happy to remain friends with her. I told her I still respected her as a person. When I woke up, I realized that I was in love with the theater girl and would do anything to have her touch me again.

As the year progressed, I became so focused on trying to make the theater girl like me that even my obsession with Magic faded into the background. I followed her around school, expounding on philosophy, fantasy art, collectible card game design, and many other topics. I often went to her house, staying until the boyfriend came over.

I didn't think the boyfriend looked like my drawing, but I envied his knowledge of computers. I briefly included "computer"-adjacent elements in my artwork, copying humanoid vehicle designs from manga and anime. I even affected a robotic, monotonous speaking cadence while talking to the theater girl, going so far as to assert to her, during a particularly charged conversation, that I was "more interested in computers than people."

I liked that the theater girl seemed interested in what I was saying. She seemed to believe it, and take it seriously. She said that I was unlike anyone else she knew. That was what I liked about her. And she was right. When I saw Ilya at this time, I told him that he had an insufficiently romantic attitude towards life, and that was why he kept losing to me at Magic.

꠵

Later that year, things got worse. When I finally confessed my feelings to the theater girl, she rejected me, saying she wasn't a lesbian, and seemed angry with me for "lying" about the nature of our relationship, as if my previous metaphorical statements about a lack of romantic interest had not actually been indicative, so I had thought, of a special intensity of romantic feeling.

I also did not get into most of the colleges I applied to, contrary to my parents' wishes. I got an "art scholarship" to an art school in New York. It was for one thousand dollars – a minuscule part of the annual tuition. My parents were, of course, angry, and there was an ugly scene where I tore up and physically swallowed some of my college applications. My mom ended up driving me to the emergency room against my will. Eventually, my parents said they would pay for the school.

My first year of college was also bad. I met a guy who introduced me to the writings of Ayn Rand. They were the only books I could focus on at the time. Their stern narratives of career and romantic success briefly stirred me from my mental suffering. Life marginally improved when I started dating the Ayn Rand guy, as did my relationship with my parents. My mom started telling people that I was "going to school in New York," like it was a major accomplishment.

At the end of my second year of college, I became embarrassed by how much my parents were paying for my school, and did not submit the tuition for the following year. I used the money to rent an apartment with the Ayn Rand guy in Queens, where we began to live together. I signed up for an online figure drawing class. We would take the Roosevelt Island tramway to Manhattan every day. We would go to the library, where I would do homework for my online figure drawing class while he studied philosophy and history using the library's free resources. We talked to each other about our projects and what we were doing. I was relieved not to be alone.

On Thanksgiving, I told my parents I could not come home because of how much I was "studying for finals." The Ayn Rand boyfriend and I then invited two of our online friends from New Jersey to the apartment. We drank Wild Turkey bourbon and I briefly passed out in the snow. My sexual encounters with the boyfriend were stilted, but seemed philosophically meaningful. I gradually started to feel better about my life.

In a sense, my greatest wish from my Magic-playing days came true. Over time, I came to believe that I really did have a special talent or genius that other people did not. It was hard to say what it was – a greater capacity, maybe, to want what I didn't have, and dream of the future. No matter how dubious my life might have become, I felt, I had a unique destiny in store just for me. And, actually, no one contributed to this sense more than Ilya.

I still went to see him whenever I came back to visit my hometown. Instead of showing him all my Magic cards, I regaled him with tales of New York life – eating a pizza someone left on the train, being sexually propositioned in public (more than back home), calling a landlord about roaches in the apartment, and other stories of that nature. The true significance of all these experiences seemed to show itself only during my conversations with Ilya, back at his parents' house. In his sarcastic commentary, I could detect envy for the worldly knowledge I had acquired, at such great (I thought) emotional cost.

5

The next time I played Magic against Ilya, I had been out of college for a long time. I was using my parents' remaining tuition money to pay for both my and the boyfriend's living expenses. Our relationship had also deteriorated by this time. I no longer felt relief when I talked to him about my projects. I ignored him and kept focusing on my art, turning some of my high school drawings into paintings that I could use to promote my as-yet-inactive sales platform on Fiverr and Etsy.

When Ilya called, I was standing in a Long Island City parking lot. For my day job, I was working for a Liberty Tax franchise, wearing a green tunic and crown to advertise tax preparation services for the upcoming tax season. It felt good to hear from him. I thought it was funny that I was doing this job, but I was also scared.

"What's happening my good bro?" I asked.

"You're visiting in a week. Let's play Magic?"

I reminded Ilya with a smirk that I had sold all my Magic cards several years ago.

"That's quite all right," said Ilya, chuckling in his annoying, semi-sarcastic way. "You do know who I work for now?"

"Uh — a different party supply store?" Ilya used to work at the Party City in our hometown.

"Rachel, my dear. You never listen to me — as usual. But that's all right."

"Maybe because your speech mannerisms are so painful to attend to, or process."

"Dude. I took those game design classes. Remember?"

"Good for you?"

"I work for Wizards of the Coast. The company that makes Magic cards? Hello?"

It turned out that his friend Alex (from Party City) helped him get hired as a support rep for *Magic: The Gathering Online*, the sole internet-based version of the game at the time. This didn't seem like an important job, but Ilya said it was, requiring encyclopedic knowledge of the rules, a willingness to engage in online debates, and an in-depth understanding of how the brand was changing. When I went to his house, he had all kinds of Magic merchandise — pre-constructed decks, themed decks, and promotional sets related to fantasy-adjacent movies and shows.

Ilya was there with his two coworkers (including Alex) as well as the younger cousin I had once so disliked (now in high school). The former high school theater girl was also there. We were now on speaking terms again, so I had invited her.

Ilya and the coworkers elaborately discussed the rules. They mentioned past games they had played, and talked about changes that negated once-popular but, in their opinion, unfair strategies. They chortled about cards that I didn't know. For some reason, I began to feel agitated and angry. I did not like the new art on the cards. The male figures were overly glistening and muscular, and the female figures stood in conventional pinup-style poses.

"Fuck the control deck," I thought. When we started playing, I decided to make a red deck to express how I felt.

I listened as Ilya and his coworkers continued talk and laugh. I thought I heard one of them express surprise at the fact that Ilya "had so many female friends." I ignored the former high school theater girl's loud enthusiasm at "finally being among real nerds." I focused on what I needed to do. The red deck had a simple strategy: to win as quickly as possible by playing the same types of cards over and over.

On my first turn against Ilya, I played a Raging Goblin and attacked immediately. On my second turn, I played a Goblin Balloon Brigade and attacked again. Then I used a Goblin Grenade to sacrifice the first goblin.

"Never flinch, never falter, never fear," I quoted from an old website.

Then Ilya played a card that made his friends glance up.

"Is that Stoneforge Mystic?" asked the other coworker loudly (his name was John).

The illustration showed a pouting woman in a skin-tight costume, prominently displaying the two compressed spheres of her breasts. "You may search your library for any Equipment card and put it into your hand," said the text on the card.

"What's an Equipment card?" I asked.

"Don't worry about it," said Ilya.

"Okay, whatever," I said, only mildly frustrated by his smug tone.

"Great advice for a new player," said Alex, the first coworker.

"Your mom is a new player," I protested.

On my third turn, I played the Angry Minotaur – another classic card from the old days, though of course it now had uglier borders (their high contrast made the copyright text easier to read). I attacked again with the Goblin Balloon Brigade. At least I was still doing damage each turn. Yet to my displeasure, on his turn Ilya played another unfamiliar card.

"Batterskull?" I read.

Ilya's cousin yelped excitedly. "They haven't banned this?!" he shouted.

"Clichéd, I know," said Ilya. "I love being clichéd."

"That's always been true of you," I said, trying to invoke the old disdain.

I needed to concentrate. The card that Ilya had just played, featuring, again, ugly Photoshopped-looking borders and generic, overly busy, pop culture-inspired, vaguely Gigeresque art (but without the sensuality of H.R. Giger's actual work), was an Equipment card. But normally such Equipment cards needed resources to be equipped, and this card didn't. It also had other features and abilities, and was threatening for other reasons.

"My ex-boyfriend used to play this game all the time," said the former high school theater girl, irrelevantly. She said the name of her high school boyfriend.

I played Lava Blast, ignoring her. I had to get rid of the inauspicious equipment.

"I'm playing Lava Blast," I reminded Ilya.

"Sorry Rachel," said Ilya.

He countered the Lava Blast, using another one of his blue cards. The former high school theater girl looked on skeptically.

"Spell Pierce," she said, reading the name of the card Ilya had used. "Attacking people with lava... I guess fantasy *can* be clichéd."

Ilya's cousin jumped up off the floor. "Well, she wasn't really playing Lava Blast to attack a *person*," said Ilya's cousin. "The keyword ability for Batterskull states that its a 'living weapon' – so not a person. So yeah, she wouldn't have been using lava to hurt 'a person' even if she had succeeded."

"Fascinating," said the former high school theater girl.

"And anyway, fire isn't the only type of damage you can do," said Ilya's cousin. He had suddenly become very talkative. "There are cards that do, like, psychic damage. Negate, unsummon— "

"Those tend to be blue-aligned spells," put in Alex.

"Shut up, everyone," I said.

On his fourth turn, Ilya proceeded to attack with the contentious Batterskull. I had no choice but to sacrifice the Angry Minotaur.

"RIP to the original chump blocker," boomed John, the louder of the two coworkers.

Ilya's cousin leapt up to play bagpipe music on the computer to mark the death of the iconic creature.

"Really funny," said Ilya after a few measures of the bag-pipe music.

"I know," said Ilya's cousin. "I'm gonna beat your clichéd Stoneblade deck."

"Can you please turn off the music?" said Ilya.

He waited for the cousin to begrudgingly comply.

"Okay, so I play Hexproof Angel," he announced. "Remember, it can't be targeted by spells or abilities."

The remainder of the game went on like this. Ilya always seemed to have better cards than I could remember previously existing, or powerful creatures, or equipment, or cards that were invulnerable to the repetitive direct damage effects that comprised the bulk of my strategy. I finally lost after seven turns.

"That was fun, I guess," I said halfheartedly.

The former high school theater girl moved closer to me.

"I'm really impressed by the people who care enough to master this game," she said, "but its kind of underwhelming? I can't believe there used to be a moral panic about it."

"Yeah, but— " I said. I looked at her. Maybe she still liked me? It looked like she was waiting for me to say something. "But, like, what happened to that sense of mysterious possibility the old cards used to have?" I asked.

Maybe one day – years from now – I could leave the Ayn Rand boyfriend for her, I speculated.

"They were like something an old civilization might make. They had the look of art made by naïve, self-taught people. You know what I mean?" I asked.

"Well, I'm going to be helping design the cards pretty soon," said Ilya. He started to talk about the workplace politics at Wizards of the Coast.

"Oh yeah," said his coworker John, loudly.

THE HOT TUB STORY

"Managing the resource of 'not feeling alone' is an important part of adult life," I remember telling the person in Philadelphia (let's call him Philadelphia for convenience). We always talked a lot about video games we had played as children, resource management games such as *SimCity* and *Crusader Kings*, so I knew he would appreciate my use of that type of language. "There are some other stats, but that's the most important one."

"Oh? What are some other 'stats'?" he asked, amused.

We had never lived together, but I had once dreamt that we – Philadelphia and I – had to share the same room, and bed, due to our poor financial circumstances as artists.

"Oh I don't know, food, money, memories," I said. "Body fat percentage?"

I looked at him. He had a good/normal body fat percentage. In the dream, I had looked down at his crotch region, which had immediately turned into, I recalled, some kind of animal – a tortoise perhaps – which then quickly (for a tortoise) walked away from our shared bed, an indicator of my shame.

⌇

Last week there was a crisis at work. Philadelphia (the person) was now getting a graduate degree in literature at the University of Pennsylvania. For a long time now – this was years after the conversation about stats – I had wanted to visit him, but had never been able to make it happen. Despite everything that had happened, or not happened, between us, I was still good friends with him, and I was attracted by the possibility of talking to him, not just about myself and what I was doing in New York, but also about him, and what he was doing in Philadelphia (the city) and how his life had turned out.

But when, two weeks ago, I had decided to act upon this desire and had messaged him and proposed that I should come to visit him in Philadelphia (the city), unfortunately, Philadelphia (the person) had told me that he was due to start teaching classes in a month, which would be very time-consuming, and therefore that the only time I could visit him in the next several months would be in the next three weeks.

This was a problem, because in order for that to happen, administratively, I would have had to have asked for a vacation at work *the week before*.

My boss, Jennifer Smith, had sent us an email – I remembered getting this email from her – saying if we wanted to have more than a week off, we should schedule it at least three weeks ahead of time. Of course, I had immediately sent her an email, but it had not been three weeks ahead of time; it had been a week less than that. And by last Tuesday, over a week after I had sent the email, she had still not gotten back to me.

Moreover, on that same day, on Tuesday, I had received an alert from the project manager saying there was a problem with our ebook reader. None of the ebooks on our website were loading. It was because the epub processing tool I had been using to build the epub packages created new IDs for each file in the epub manifest, but the website expected the IDs to stay the same. Now, the IDs weren't staying the same and the website, the ebook part of the website, wasn't working.

Worse, I seemed to have caused the problem. I had hoped to be able to use the epub processing tool to speed up the process of creating the remaining ebooks, so that I would then have been justified in asking Jennifer Smith for a vacation a week-or-so past the three-week lead-up time that she had suggested in her email. Now that was no longer possible. And, in fact, nothing seemed possible. I began to have suicidal ideation. I wanted to die.

Then, suddenly, the crisis was over. On Thursday, two other developers on the project, Joachim del Canto and Mike Miller, came into the office. They were sympathetic to my explanation of the changing IDs problem with the epub processing tool. They commiserated with me about the frustrations of working in IT, and, without noticing it, I soon found myself naturally participating in an animated three-person discussion about politics, movies, and pop culture. I felt better.

Later, I went into the stairwell by myself and took a picture of the hole inside going down fifteen floors, to which I added the caption "office hole!" when I posted it on social media. I suddenly felt able to follow up with Jennifer Smith about going to Philadelphia, without risk of creating problems at work. Maybe I would not even need to visit Philadelphia (the person, not the city, or rather both) in order to feel good.

The improvement in my situation continued on Friday, when, after work, I was able to go to a bar with Joachim del Canto and Mike Miller. It was my first time socializing like this outside the office, informally, rather than as part of an official "happy hour" organized by workers with whom I had not previously participated in a movies/politics type of discussion, as I now had with Joachim del Canto and Mike Miller. After my second vodka soda, I shared with my coworkers the main drama of my life. It related to a third thing that had been on my mind, in addition to the ebook crisis and the unresolved question of the vacation to Philadelphia (the city, not the person, or rather both): I had a literary reading scheduled during the upcoming week at this one gay bar, in Brooklyn. I had wanted to be an "artist type" back when I was young, to compensate for the indignities I faced in school and elsewhere. Being an "artist type" would, as I imagined it then, be like in that movie *Good Will Hunting*, except the thing that I would be good at would be writing, not math (and I would be trans). And now, in fact, I had become one of the people who had been invited to read at a monthly series for local LGBTQ storytellers and performers. Mike Miller and Joachim del Canto showed excitement in response to this information. They verbalized an interest in and support for my plans.

"Maybe we can even come to the reading!" said Mike Miller.

"Haha, well, it is for a certain demographic," I said.

But I was secretly pleased by their support.

꙳

On Saturday, I messaged Philadelphia (the person). I told him I would not be able to visit him at the agreed-upon time. I had realized I could not be in Philadelphia (the city) until Wednesday at the earliest, because the reading in Brooklyn was scheduled for Tuesday. I could not understand how I could have forgotten this. Moreover, there was now no time, I realized, to even worry about the fact I was now not going on vacation. I had been so preoccupied with my problems at work, and their climactic resolution on Friday night, that I had not begun to write the story that I was supposed to read at that reading, which promised to be, on the whole, a more potent solution to the problem of "not feeling alone" than the Philadelphia trip. For if I succeeded attracting positive attention from the people at that bar when I read that story, then that person – *not* the person in Philadelphia, but a different person, a person in Brooklyn (like that bar) – would probably hear about it.

The person in Brooklyn was someone with whom I had tried, and failed, to initiate a romantic relationship (we can, provisionally and inadequately, call her Brooklyn for convenience, though it is a bad name that does not convey the intensity of my feelings). Whatever else happened, Brooklyn (the person) would inevitably hear my name spoken in the days after the LGBTQ storytelling event by the people who were sure to have been there – either Avery, or Jim, or Sophia. She (Brooklyn) would know I had read there, at the LGBTQ storytelling event, with other people, and that I had not felt alone.

I spent the whole weekend trying to work on the story. It was surprisingly difficult.

I went through every anecdote and memory I had, any incident that could possibly be of interest to the people who were going to be at that bar, listening to LGBTQ storytellers and performers. I wrote down anything that involved sex, or being awkward, or just any memory that I had any feelings about that revealed any interesting autobiographical facts about me.

I wondered if I should write about the person I had sex with in high school; or the time I watched porn; or the time I was on a camping trip and saw people having sex. I considered writing about how Philadelphia (the person) one time, when we both lived in Texas, drove from San Marcos to Fredericksburg and then came back and talked to me passionately and morosely about old video games – both *Crusader Kings* and *SimCity*. Philadelphia had gone into minute detail about the games' resource management mechanics, and we both admired the games' philosophically naive, upbeat, yet unflinching, clockwork-like depiction of futile human activity.

I considered the tedious background question of whether I had been "attracted to him" or "felt nothing" – whether I should have gone into his apartment to work on games, what I would have gotten out of that. But no, I could already tell that was too boring. Or rather: It was counterproductive to try to play up those old feelings in this new context.

Ultimately, I settled on the hot tub story. This was not a good story from a "plot" standpoint. But I remembered telling it to a man that I had had sex with last year, which had made it seem significant. Was the story also significant in itself, apart from my having told it to that man? Possibly. I reflected on the fact that I had liked the interaction of telling the man the story more than I had liked the interaction of having sex with the man. This latter interaction (like many others) had been strenuous, performative, ambiguous, and confusing.

I concluded that the hot tub story would probably have the same effect on the people at the gay bar that it had on that man: that is, of causing them to be interested in what I was saying in a way that also suggested that I was desirable as a person. In this way, I thought, my whole being, my whole essence, would be communicated indirectly to that person, Brooklyn (not the city), when she heard about my having read the hot tub story at the LGBTQ storytelling event – even though she herself was likely to be absent from the event.

⌖

On Monday, two days ago, I was at work. I looked at the story-telling event's Facebook page. I looked for any discrepancy between the number of people who were reported as "interested" in the event and the number of actual profiles I was able to count in the column of "interested" people. There were 21 "interested" people, yet I could only see 20 Facebook profiles in the "interested" column. This meant that Brooklyn, who had blocked me on Facebook, had marked herself as "interested" in the event.

I sent my boss an email, not about the vacation to Philadelphia (the city) (an idea that I had conclusively abandoned) but about our FTP server credentials. In this way, I attempted to establish that I did not care about the vacation at all; that both it and my untimely request had been completely effaced from my mind by work-related matters such as the FTP server, and that, in fact, my lack of interest in the vacation was the reason that my request for it had been so short-notice in the first place.

On Tuesday, yesterday, the day of the LGBTQ story-telling event, I did not do any work. I could not stop thinking about Brooklyn. At 3 p.m. I sent two Facebook messages, one to Philadelphia and one to Bev — a third person, with whom I have a whole separate history, and to whom I had told the whole story of how Brooklyn blocked me and how I felt about that. The two Facebook messages consisted of a screenshot of my browser, opened to a web page where users can send anonymous text messages. The implication was that the recipient of the anonymous message would get it, even if they had blocked my phone number.

"Come to my show tonight at the eagle :) - you know who this is," said the as-yet-unsent message.

"Should I send this???" I asked both Bev and Philadelphia.

Philadelphia did not answer. He was probably in class. I had found that, during the past eight months of my fixation with Brooklyn, he had not been able to offer me much advice. Last year, he had married another LGBTQ person/putative academic, and had become less interested in my problems.

Bev answered after a while. "Doesn't she already know you are in this reading?" she asked.

"Yeah, but that's not the point. I definitely, definitely don't want her to come to the reading." My hands were shaking. "I don't want her to come to the reading," I repeated.

"Yeah, your best-case scenario is not that great," answered Bev.

"You don't understand," I wrote to Bev. "Sorry I am being so weird and passionate about this haha."

I sent her a series of long and short messages:

"One time I was looking at her Facebook page."

"I mean with my other account because as you know she blocked me haha."

"She said that she likes being on stage. She said it feels like having sex. You don't understand. That is ALSO how it feels to me. That is JUST how it feels to me, also."

"You were in the hot tub with me. Oh yeah by the way, I am gonna be reading that hot tub story tonight, so sorry if I'm gonna be exploiting our experience together."

"Haha," said Bev, responding to the last of my messages. "I'm sure it will be great! It was that time with Jurgen."

"Yes exactly haha."

"I don't even remember what happened!"

※

The performance was starting at seven. At 6:00 p.m. I was still trying to decide whether or not to send Brooklyn (the person) the anonymous text message. I finally decided to do it. This was not so that Brooklyn would go to the performance — something that, given my understanding of why she was shunning me and the likely outcomes of the situation for myself, I concluded that I ultimately did not want — but so that she would see the message from me and be forced to wonder about it, and be unable to do anything to stop herself from wondering. She really was just like me in this way. Maybe she would even think it was attractive that I knew this much about her, and cared enough, and was tactical enough, to try to emotionally destabilize her like this.

At 6:40 p.m., sitting on the front steps of the bar, I used my phone to click Send on the text messaging website.

At 6:45 p.m. I started to wonder whether or not she had received the message. On the website, I had had to type in the name of her mobile service provider, which I had found via another site. I wondered if I had entered the name of the wrong mobile service provider. I tested it out by trying to send myself a text message, giving the name of my own mobile service provider. I waited for three to five minutes. I did not get the message. I tried a different anonymous text messaging website. It still did not work. At 6:55 p.m. I finally found an anonymous text messaging website that did work when I tested it out using the above method. Using this other website, I sent Brooklyn (the person) a third, and final, message.

The message said: "Come to my show tonight at the eagle :) - you know who this is - sorry if u got multiple messages, phone is messed up :)"

At 7 p.m. I entered the bar. My coworkers were not present, which was a relief. I was hoping that the excitement that I was feeling in connection with Brooklyn, her past validation of me, the apparent (but perhaps, I thought, false) reality of her present rejection, would translate into an effective telling of the hot tub story. I listened to a man tell a story about having sex with a man. I listened to another man read a story about being transgender. Then it was my turn. I faced the audience of ten to fifteen people who were there for the reading.

"Okay, so, this is the hot tub story," I said into the mic.

There had not been enough time to actually write the story. I had no choice but to tell it to the people directly, relying on the same innate storytelling ability I had demonstrated with the man with whom I had had sex back in April.

"So, what happened was this. I was at my parents' house in California. This was about two years ago. They just got this house, and it was this whole thing, this drama of them getting the house. Like *The Great Gatsby*!" I said, referring to both the book and the character. "Then a person came over, let's call her Bev, for convenience. And I have this whole history with her. A romantic history, you could say! But that was long before we were in the hot tub together so it doesn't matter."

The man I had sex with last year, I realized, had asked questions when I told him the story. That was why, by the time I was telling him this part of it, the hot tub part, he already knew who these people were. But that was not going to happen here.

"Okay," I continued. "So then we invited our other friend over, Jurgen. And she and I, Bev, both have this whole history with him, with Jurgen. But, also, I have a totally different history with Jurgen than Bev does. But for both of us, our history with him was partially informed by our history with each other, but not completely. And, even now, I have a totally different perception of this dude than Bev. And I also had a very different perception of him then."

I looked at Jim and Avery and Sophia. Their faces were sympathetic, expectant. That the hot tub story might not come together now, any more than it had when I was thinking about it on Saturday, Sunday, Monday, or earlier today, was a possibility that had occurred to me earlier but which I had previously dismissed.

"There are a lot of elements to this story," I continued. "In addition to this drama of the family, with its undercurrent of like, uh, sadness and, uh, death."

I tried to think of at least one element from the story.

"So, in addition to all these story elements, there was, uh – well, there was Jurgen, okay."

I focused on the flattering, depersonalized sound of my microphone-amplified voice. It did, it definitely did remind me of sex, of Brooklyn (the person), of what I thought I could achieve, of what I thought sex was, or could be. A woman you really like shows you your best version of yourself, I thought. I just needed to tell them about Jurgen.

"I have thought of one thing about Jurgen. I have thought of a representative anecdote about Jurgen."

"Hold the mic closer," suggested Sophia.

"Okay," I said. I looked straight at the audience. "So, uh, when I was in college. This is the anecdote about Jurgen, by the way. So, uh, in college, I was really depressed, okay. But, also, I was going to UCLA. And this dude, Jurgen – so, as I said I have a whole other history with him, and this is, like, part of that history – so, anyway, this dude would sometimes ride his motorcycle to LA. And we would hang out. And I had a motorcycle at that time too, by the way."

People nodded.

"And then this girl I hated," I continued, "this girl from UCLA I mean, my roommate, not Bev in the hot tub, that's a totally different story, haha — anyway, this annoying girl from UCLA — let's call her UCLA for convenience — even thought that he was my boyfriend! But anyway, that is not the story.",

I paused.

"And okay, so, the REAL story is, sometimes on the weekends Jurgen and I would hang out and stuff — with his motorcycle. And it was always his initiative, okay. Well, maybe not always?" I ventured. "But anyway, we would have these conversations that were pointless in this very specific way, you know? All alienated and shit."

I held the microphone so close it was touching my mouth.

"These pointless, alienated conversations about nothing that go nowhere!" I yelled. "Because he was such an angsty, alienated guy. He grew up in Latvia, you know, with all these stories of when it was still the Soviet Union. As did I. Well, not Latvia, but St. Petersburg. But that was still part of the Soviet Union," I concluded at a lower volume.

There was a pause as I tried to figure out how to continue from there. After a while, someone asked:

"Where was the hot tub?"

It was Sophia.

"Haha, hang on," I answered.

I was still thinking. I was trying to weigh the importance of the Jurgen/motorcycle story relative to the larger narrative I was trying to impart.

"Was it at your parents' house?"

"Yes! But I still have not finished the anecdote about Jurgen."

I finally decided to continue with the portion of the narrative about UCLA (the university).

"Did you at least make out with your friend?" asked Sophia.

"No! And its more complicated than that!"

"I just want to know who was in the hot tub with you!"

I could tell she was trying to help.

"Haha I will get to it!" I said, affecting a bratty, childish tone.

At last, I finished telling the anecdote about Jurgen. It was about how he'd wanted to crash his motorcycle when we were in college. Or, rather, it was about how he talked about wanting to crash his motorcycle – "not in a suicidal way!" I assured the audience.

"He merely talked about what it would be like, 'in a neutral way,'" I said.

That was how he had put it. Failing to turn on a mountain road, deciding, or failing to decide, to put his weight fully into the turn, how "cool" and "interesting" that was, that something so small, such a small change in his actions, could have such a drastic effect on reality.

"That was just the kind of thing he would talk about. And he'd always talk about being 'a scientist' in this stupid way. He was one of those math and science guys who had a whole identity about being 'logical.' That was something that was so annoying about him..."

In the end, I thought that the anecdote about Jurgen went reasonably well. Or, rather, it did not go well, but that was also an acceptable outcome, well within the range of what I was able to tolerate. I knew that what is termed "cringe" – a visceral pain, suggesting adolescence, the vulnerability and emotions stemming from that — was seen as part of my "brand" as an LGBTQ storyteller and performer. Due to unavoidable circumstances, I had been forced to play up that part of my identity during the performance — and, perhaps, that had been enough. Unfortunately, and this was why I had to make a long, unhappy Facebook post at work the next day (that is, earlier today), after I finished telling the part about Jurgen, I ran out of time.

Jim began to turn the lights on and off.

"I am not done!" I yelled — trying, still, to at least start talking about the hot tub.

"Jurgen actually wanted to die!" I said. I spoke quickly. "He was sad and, uh — interested, I guess — in the romance of death. He was actually depressed! But I still didn't like him! That's the whole point of the anecdote," I shouted when the host, not Sophia but another person, her friend, walked onto the stage. I still did not see my coworkers anywhere. I did not have time to get to the hot tub part of the story.

After the reading, Jim and Avery and Sophia did not talk to me, and the person who blocked me (who I have been referring to as Brooklyn, for convenience) was not there.

AUGUST, 1962

"Dave looks a little tense," said President John F. Kennedy. "Why don't you help him out?"

Samuel Beckett, wearing a fashionable striped swimsuit, looked at the smiling presidential aide swinging his legs in the indoor pool, which was heated to almost the exact temperature of the human body. Kennedy playfully placed a hand on his ass, as if nudging him forward through the water, and Sam turned around to consider once more the president's thin, handsome features, the boyish, pursed lips, the heavy-lidded eyes filled with the joy of competition.

He knew that it was sometime in August of 1962. He didn't know exactly how long he had been inhabiting this particular role. Ever since the president had maneuvered him into Jackie Kennedy's bedroom and had quick, workmanlike sex with him, thinking that Sam was a naïve female college intern instead of man of science who was chosen by God to be the "eternally recurring hero" of history by mystically "leaping" into different bodies in time and space in order to save the people of twentieth-century America – ever since that moment, Sam Beckett was completely absorbed by the sensory and emotional reality of his new life.

He told himself that there were personal reasons for doing what he was doing. He remembered the Kennedy presidency from his own, distant childhood, long before he began the groundbreaking theoretical work that would lead to creation of the Quantum Leap project. He remembered the hopeful feelings everyone had, the freedom marches, the promise of a man on the moon, all that stuff.

He remembered watching the youngish man with the full head of hair and bold smile talk articulately on television, feeling vaguely tragic and guilty over the fact that his mother and father, who were the nicest people he knew, didn't understand. He felt then that the man on television, beloved, criticized, admired, was the only one who was *like him*, in a fundamental way. The feeling stayed with him, on and off, through his childhood and adolescence. He cried, secretly, when Kennedy was shot, not because he was sad but because he knew that it was going to happen and was emotionally overwhelmed.

The president stuck his finger between the two halves of Sam's ass, which was covered by the fabric of his swimsuit. Kennedy laughed a little, waving in the direction of his aide, a pale, decent, balding man who gamely shrugged his shoulders and gave them an encouraging smile from where he was sitting at the pool's edge. It was what made the president feel alive. Sam knew that he wasn't obligated to give the presidential aide, Dave Powers, oral sex; but he wanted to. The tragic, inspiring feeling from his childhood was mixed up with these sensations.

"Oh, well, you don't need to – that's very nice of you," said Dave Powers, as Sam pulled down the man's swim trunks and put his semi-erect penis in his mouth. Sam felt Kennedy behind him in the pool, watching him, assessing the scene, probably, with the same kind of restless satisfaction with which he had watched the electoral votes coming in against Nixon. He hoped that Kennedy would still want to have sex with him later in the evening, instead of becoming overcome with remorse for what he was making him do now.

Suddenly, he heard the distinctive whoosh of the holographic chamber door opening, indicating the arrival of Al from the project.

"Oh my god Sam," said the voice of his best friend, a voice somehow still familiar after all these days or months. "I can't see what you're doing. I don't want to know. I am deliberately standing in such a way as to avoid seeing or knowing."

Sam ignored the voice and concentrated on the sensation of fellating Kennedy's aide, the penis assuming its full, evilly majestic form in his mouth.

"Listen," shouted Al, agitated. "You can't keep doing this – uh, whatever it is," he trailed off. "You have to figure out what it is that you're trying to do in this time period. The project is gonna lose funding, you can't— "

Al swore as he thumped his handheld communication device. It emitted a series of angry whirrs and beeps, which interrupted the feelings of voluptuous self-abnegation Sam was experiencing.

"Maybe what I'm trying to do," said Sam finally, taking his mouth off the aide's genitalia, "is show this man there is no shame in submission."

"You stopped," said Dave Powers. "That's good," he added weakly.

"The heroes we love the most," continued Sam, cradling the base of the man's penis, "are not the masters of history, but its instruments, its martyrs – Martin Luther King, Joan of Arc."

"What *are* you talking about?" said Al.

Sam thought he could hear Kennedy moving in behind him, maybe to protect him – maybe just straining to hear what was being said. Sam thought of having his body penetrated, used, pushed down or against a wall in countless conference rooms, offices, and hotel bedrooms, all for the comfort and existential reassurance of the man who himself vaingloriously sought to reassure the nation.

His will and his body – like those of Kennedy – were not his own, but belonged to something greater than himself – to God, to History – some terrible, nameless, unfathomable thing. It was an erotic sensation. He felt a blue light filling his body. Maybe this would be the leap home.

CASSANDRA

Dan stopped answering my messages just as I started to think that maybe my campaign for US Congress was about to go somewhere. Dan's old graduate adviser, F. F., a famous author and activist, had nominated me to be one of the candidates funded by Brand New Congress, a nationwide organization that helped hundreds of progressive candidates without establishment backing, such as myself. If selected, my campaign would be given a huge platform, and maybe I could win. And I actually felt like I could do it. I had done many things like this before. I had gone through the paperwork to change my name. I had changed my appearance. I had gone to a tech boot camp and had gotten a tech job. This felt, in the end, like the same type of project. All I had to do now was do enough research to know what issues I wanted to talk about and what I could fix, and I had begun this process too.

"It's just a question of willpower and leveraging your male privilege" — that is how I once jokingly put it to Dan. So it was ironic that Dan, who was the one who solidified my perception of myself as a certain type of man, the type of man who would say that, was ignoring my messages.

"Hang out with me bro, I'm so lonely," I texted him.

"Just kidding bro," I texted again after a while.

"Is everything OK bro?"

"Sorry didn't mean to sound overly concerned – didn't mean to 'concern troll' you into replying, haha," I wrote finally.

But Dan did not reply. The status indicator next to the messages kept saying "delivered," but not "seen," implying that he had seen the messages but not committed to opening them on his phone. I wondered about the subtext of the messages.

In the past month, just as our campaign was starting to get traction, as the video of me insulting my opponent Jonathan Bing by saying that he was "a tool in the most literal sense" started to be shared on the internet, as our AMA thread got more than 200 upvotes and was briefly at the top of the page, as it looked (based on our fake petitions) like we'd be very likely to exceed the minimum number of 1,250 designating petitions next year, Dan had been participating less and less.

Maybe he was depressed again. Or were my repeated messages making him feel as if I, the servant, had begun to supplant the master? Was that how I felt?

The graduate adviser who had nominated me to Brand New Congress had invited me to address the book club that met at her apartment. They discussed books about history and social policy, so she said it would make sense for me to talk to the people there afterwards. I was going to give a short presentation about the housing crisis in America's cities, and the policies I would try to push through Congress to resolve it.

I was excited for the chance to make the speech, and anxious for Dan to be there — not just to hear me talk about our plans, but also to provide a buffer between me and the other people at the book club.

I still found it hard to engage with people one on one. Despite all the work I have done on myself — by attending all those Grindr and OkCupid dates, as well as at the more conventional political activist meetings and networking events — that was the one thing that remained. I used to worry this might disqualify me somehow — wanting to represent a subset of the US population when I had so much trouble relating to its members as individuals. I have since realized that many leaders have probably had that problem. Lyndon Johnson probably had that problem. Dan was in the middle of a big Lyndon Johnson obsession when we last spoke, and I had made that observation to him. He had even agreed.

"Help, that lesbian professor invited me to her apartment!" I texted Dan.

"Should I have said 'lesbian'?" I added, seeing no answer from him. I could not help myself. "It sounds like a very 2005 term!" Finally, I wrote: "Wait, was that book club thing at 7 or 8? I thought you would know!"

Still no reply.

I stared at the wall of books I used as a backdrop whenever I posted videos to social media. Plato's *Republic*, *Paradise Lost*, Machiavelli's *The Prince*, and other generic classics that I had bought after college. I still have not read most of those books. The sight of all those titles, which evoked the loneliness of those past days, prompted me to follow up my message to Dan with an ironic heart symbol. I sent it to, again, no effect.

Finally, on the actual day the book club was supposed to be meeting, I got a message from Dan's girlfriend. This was not Rachel or Medea, but a different woman, though she still had a mythological name.

"Meet up at 6? For the book club," said the message.

I remembered seeing her, this specific woman, in the audience of a comedy show at a local gay bar that Dan's friends liked to go to. She had long hair and was conventionally good-looking, and had shown her vociferous support for the comedian via aggressive laughter and clapping. I was, I admitted to myself, anxious about the prospect of a one-on-one encounter with her. She had been rude to me at the bar, and now she was Dan's girlfriend.

～5～

However when we met up, she was not rude to me. She was actually nice. She looked at me attentively as I sat across from her at the outdoor table of the restaurant.

"The man of the hour," she announced.

"That's me!" I said. Despite myself, I moved with nervous energy. "Maybe soon I'll be the man of the decade. With your help, hahaha."

"Aw, I know you will," said Dan's girlfriend.

She looked directly at me in a theatrical way. She wore red cat-eye glasses, but her eyes — large and blue — were clearly perceptible behind the thin lenses.

"I can see right away that you're a very charming man."

"You think so? Is that what Dan said about me?" I asked immediately. "Did he say I'm charming?"

She faltered briefly in her mock-seductive gaze. She seemed to think about what to say.

"Well, Dan says you're a homosexual."

"Hahaha," I answered. "Well, that's true to an extent."

If that was how the meeting was going, if she thought I was important enough as Dan's friend to jokingly make fun of, I was willing to meet her at that level.

"I guess its more that I just don't like women," I said, lightly.

"You're disgusting," she said, lighting a cigarette.

I nodded happily in agreement.

She took a large drag of the cigarette. The glasses made her look like an attractive actress in a teen coming-of-age movie playing a "nerd" character. I thought of my engagements with Chris and the other men from the internet, how unsatisfactory they were as "dates" in the purely conventional sense. I obviously wasn't here to talk to her about that.

Dan's girlfriend looked demonstratively for a place to ash the cigarette. There was something about her overly animated manner, the way she pointedly engaged with the cigarette and fussily tapped on it, that made me feel superior to her and also made me want her to see my superiority.

"Maybe I kind of do like women, in a fucked-up way," I said.

Dan's girlfriend raised an eyebrow, contorting her whole face in an expression of whimsical skepticism.

She so clearly wanted to be the center of attention, both in the moment, in whatever interaction she was having, and in the broader social world, I thought. Even at the comedy show, she had somehow made the performance be about her, her approval of the performer. Of course, trans women were always like this, always actively "taking up space" as women — such a stark contrast to what I remembered as being expected of me growing up as a woman — but she was the most like this of any of them. In a way, I could see why Dan would like her.

I continued to explicate the nature of my interest in women.

"But my fucked-up interest doesn't apply to trans women," I told her. "The problem is, trans women aren't fucked-up *enough*. What's fucked up about being a woman is that this status is inflicted on you. A humiliation. If you *choose* to be a woman, are you really being a woman? I mean, probably you are," I corrected myself, "but it still doesn't do anything for me. Just be one thing, haha."

I was saying a prepared statement, something I had often thought or articulated to myself before. But her whole expression changed. She pushed her chair back, as if she was about to stand up and leave.

"Sorry, you're actually being transphobic."

"Huh? What?"

In spite of myself, I was taken aback by the change, which, again, transformed her whole face into a mask of revulsion or even, perhaps, fear. I had gotten used to the impression of interest in me she had been projecting, artificial as that, too, had perhaps been. Maybe it was actually my sense of her interest in me, rather than my judgment over her, that had inspired me to talk like this.

"To reiterate, I think its valid to be whatever gender you want!" I said, eager to make her like me again. "Trans women *are* valid as women. If anything, the problem is they are too wholesome— "

She still looked cold. It really felt like a wall had come down.

"I was merely talking about my own personal preferences, which are quite twisted, admittedly," I said. I affected an injured dignity. "You asked me, and I told you."

"Well, actually no one asked you," said Dan's girlfriend.

At that point, the waiter appeared – a thin, conventionally attractive man Dan's girlfriend began to elaborately negotiate with on our behalf, asking whether he cared if she smoked, leaping to his assistance when he began to position objects on the rickety, too-small table. "I hope your day has been good!" she said, giving him a slight smile.

I remained engrossed in thought.

"What would you like – Ashton? I am ordering for both of us," she informed the waiter.

"Uhh, food? Actually, a vodka soda thanks."

Dan's girlfriend glanced at me – I thought, slightly sympathetically. "Yes, I'll have one as well."

Was it possible that her contempt for me had diminished? Did she think it was meaningful that we both ordered the same low-calorie drink?

"I'm sorry," I said. "I was being really flippant. And maybe if an individual trans woman is fucked-up enough— "

"I wanted to leave, but he was already here," she interrupted me, referring to the still-present waiter. "I didn't want to waste his time. Service worker solidarity."

"Yes of course," I said.

᧔

Soon after this, Dan's girlfriend got a message from Dan. She frowned and began to reply immediately, typing quickly into her phone. They corresponded for some time. The girlfriend's annoyance with me seemed to finally recede into the background as she became preoccupied with answering the series of messages. Her face, which had been so animated, became still with concentration, and the light reflected off her glasses as she typed. She really did now look studious and considerate. I could see where her jawline had probably become more feminine over time, giving an impression of subtle vulnerability.

She looked up at me. "Ugh, Dan's really worried about this book club event."

"Oh wow, he didn't say anything about it to me."

"You can't keep track of your own events? You must be so disorganized—"

She shook her head disparagingly. But, again, her energy now seemed to be fully dedicated to the absent Dan and their correspondence.

"I mean, he didn't say anything about being worried," I retorted.

I paused, then decided to assume a sensitive tone.

"We actually haven't talked in over a month. Even though he's supposed to be managing my whole campaign."

Saying this felt good, better than I would have thought. It felt good to earnestly confess my sadness to somebody – a sort of feminine figure – who might listen.

Dan's girlfriend put away her phone.

"You sound sad."

"Well, yes," I said, encouraged. "I feel sad."

"I guess you really do care about him."

She was looking straight at me. She wasn't being sarcastic. "Is he like – depressed? I remember being depressed."

"It's complicated. He's a very complicated man. Ugh."

This utterance was also unironic. I saw that she, too, actually cared about Dan. I thought about the two of them together, the type of relationship they might have. He was high-minded and influential. He would probably be able to provide her with the unwavering, almost parental attention that she was always overtly and covertly demanding. And there would be a sexual component as well. He had told me once, in the park, that he thought of a strap-on as a tool, "like an electric sander," rather than an extension of his body.

"Well, if it helps, you just have to keep doing stuff," I said after a while. "You have to stay active and engaged, even if you feel like it doesn't matter. That's what you should tell him."

"God knows I try. I'm doing my best as his girlfriend."

I drank my vodka soda. I was suddenly moved by the word "girlfriend."

"Well, you know, he was the one who originally got me out of being depressed," I said.

"Really?" she asked. She was looking directly at me. It seemed she wasn't annoyed with me anymore.

"Yeah! He has a way of always acting interested in the person he's talking to, and I guess that really inspired me. And he seemed really interested in me, my ideas."

I took another large sip of my drink.

"And his *way* of listening – that is rare too. Active listening. That takes real talent, to be able to really *see* a person, like he *saw* me. To ask the right questions. That is something I want to emulate, as a politician. Sorry, I'm being too earnest right now."

But his girlfriend seemed to, also, be listening. "No, I like that you're earnest," she said. "Everyone's too fake these days."

"Yes," I agreed. "Maybe you're right."

I continued my speech in praise of Dan. I wanted her to see me earnestly saying what I believed.

"I could see how angry he was too. I mean, about what was happening in the world. Getting so obsessed with local elections after 2016. Getting so obsessed with Carolyn Maloney, her not running for re-election, why that's bad. I could make a whole speech about that — and I have, haha. But anyway."

I paused.

"I think he is angry about the past," I said. "His past."

I finished what was left of my drink.

"We all have sad pasts, you know," I told her.

"Mm," she nodded. She sipped on her own drink. Then her phone made its now-familiar notification sound. She frowned at the incoming message. She looked up.

"So, uh — I think we have to go back to my place. Before the book club."

"Okay," I replied absentmindedly.

I was still thinking about what I had just said. I thought of Dan's girlfriend comforting him. Him dealing with the shameful weight of his female past. Them acting out, together, those fraught, heterosexual roles.

"Wait, isn't your place kind of far from here?" I remembered.

"Yeah, we have to be quick," she said.

She stood up.

"Can you, like – pay?" she asked.

She handed me the check.

She lightly brushed my shoulder as she walked past.

〜5〜

As the J train clattered over the bridge into Brooklyn, Dan's girlfriend let me see some of his messages.

"My issue with F.," he had written, "is that she's gonna do her thing like always."

He still referred to the woman at the book club by her first initial, even though they were no longer, apparently, in personal contact. I looked around. The train was crowded with rush hour passengers, but we were able to find seats. We were sitting together. I leaned over Dan's girlfriend's shoulder to read her messages.

"She will talk about non-profits, she will talk about community boards, she will not look at what can be done to implement change on a big level, she does not want to see that," said Dan's next message.

The screen was chaotic with other unread messages and notifications.

"We're running for US Congress here!", Dan had written. "We are going to pass the laws that will basically bring socialism to the US. You have to make sure Ashton is clear on that point. I trust you to do this."

"Yes, father," Dan's girlfriend had answered.

In response, there was an emoji of a fist – colored pale pink, to specifically represent "Caucasian" skin, instead of the default yellow – moving towards the screen.

"Haha," I said. "Is that like a sex thing? I mean the fist."

"Hahaha," said Dan's girlfriend.

She laughed exaggeratedly, out of proportion to the supposed humor of my statement, then shoved me, hard enough that I violently collided with the person sitting on the other side of me on the train. I looked up to see a young, hard-jawed man dressed in conservative, casual clothes. He wore a windproof bomber jacket (I had once considered buying a similar jacket) and flat-brimmed hat with a sports team logo on it — the Yankees.

Dan's girlfriend apologized immediately.

"It's cool," said the man. He looked at us for some time. "You okay?" he finally asked Dan's girlfriend.

Before he could do or say anything else, she immediately began to narrate our evening to him, looking directly into his eyes, gesturing wildly.

"You have to watch out for him, he's like literally spineless," she said. She put her arm around me. "Did you know, when we were having drinks, the waiter instinctively asked me to order for us?" she asked.

I could not resist contradicting her. "No way," I said. "That is totally not true."

Despite my supposedly exclusive preference, now, for men, it felt good to be seen like this — as a man on an outing with a frantic woman — by this earnest, strapping onlooker, and by, perhaps, everyone on this train, these representatives of mainstream norms.

"Maybe *you* ordered for us because you wanted to insert yourself into the waiter-customer interaction, but he gave *me* the actual check," I said.

Dan's girlfriend drew closer to me. "He gave *me* the check," she said, patting my thigh. "He put the check on *my* half of the table, and you paid for it after I asked nicely." She smiled at me.

"You all are cute," assented the man.

He watched us for a moment.

"Hey— " He paused again.

"Do you guys know where to find the Parking Lot? Like what stop?"

The Parking Lot was the name of a gay bar in the area. It was actually the same bar that Dan's friends all went to – the same one where I had first seen Dan's girlfriend attending the comedy show featuring gay and trans artists.

Dan's girlfriend disengaged herself from me.

"No," she answered emphatically. "We're not gay."

"Oh okay, chill out," said the man. I thought I saw him smirk.

"Fuck you!" said Dan's girlfriend.

"She's a feisty one," said the man.

"Why don't you pay us to help you find the gay bar?" said Dan's girlfriend.

The man looked questioningly at me. "What does she want?" he asked.

"We're not talking to you," said Dan's girlfriend.

I moved incrementally closer to Dan's girlfriend, creating a symbolic barrier between her and the man. I was trying to signify my solidarity with her, while also fulfilling my conventionally masculine, protective role, taking responsibility for her actions. I nodded at the man. He looked away, acquiescing to my non-verbal message.

Finally, he got off the train.

"By the way, I hate the Yankees," Dan's girlfriend shouted after him.

After the doors closed, she spread her arms over the back of the seat, occupying the newly available space. I felt the fabric of her oversized Members Only jacket touching the back of my neck. I did not say anything.

"Ugh, I hate men," said Dan's girlfriend. "You don't know what its like to live with the constant threat of violence."

"Hm," I said sympathetically.

I continued to sit next to her. The other people on the train, I assumed, probably still thought we were, in some way, a heterosexual couple.

"Well, actually, I do know – I do have some experience of," I started to say.

Dan's girlfriend interrupted me. "I honestly don't care."

She now looked somber. Behind the stylized frames of her glasses, her eyes looked bigger than ever – almost like a character from a nineties space anime, but more feminine, sentimental and expressive.

"I didn't 'choose' to be a woman," said Dan's girlfriend.

I considered the implications of this. I felt emboldened by my earlier performance with the man.

"Well, I guess that makes you a fucked-up enough woman for me!" I said, and patted the top her leg, imitating her gesture from earlier.

To my surprise, she did not recoil from my action.

⌇

We sat in silence as the train passed the further Brooklyn stations. We got off just before Broadway Junction, far from the book club. It was a busy area filled with small churches and pharmacies, which figured prominently in my upcoming speech about housing. A lot of the younger people I knew lived here with roommates – including, presumably, Dan's girlfriend. The latter kept checking her phone. I asked her about the timing of our outing.

"Doesn't the book club start at seven?"

"It's fine. The discussion doesn't start until eight. She knows people have jobs."

"Can we even make it by eight?"

It was, at that moment, seven. The sky above the train tracks was a promising shade of light blue. I considered leaving Dan's girlfriend behind in Bushwick and taking the train back.

"Why are we going to your apartment again?" I asked.

"I already texted her, I told her we'd be there at eight thirty," Dan's girlfriend replied to my first question.

"I didn't realize you had her number."

"Yeah, well, she and Dan aren't talking right now," said Dan's girlfriend.

She walked purposefully down the street.

"Wow," I offered.

Even though F.F. had nominated me to be funded and trained by a major political organization, she had only ever communicated with me by email. Dan and his girlfriend were clearly in closer contact with her than that.

"They still support each other's projects. I have to help him with the communication aspect of things," she explained.

She walked up the steps of a two-story building. I followed her.

"Men are somewhat lacking in the emotional intelligence department," she observed.

"Haha, very true."

I remembered how I had felt with Dan. The feeling that I — that we — were uniquely positioned to change the world, that we could actually do what no one else thought of to do, if only we talked and researched and put in enough effort. For all her exaggerated posturing, Dan and his girlfriend were meaningfully partaking in that idea.

The inside of the building was dark. We walked up a narrow stairway into a dim living room without any notice-able windows or available chairs. The room was dominated visually by a table stacked with pizza boxes — a typical col-lective apartment. It was very different, of course, from Dan's place, with its carefully spaced modern furniture and framed posters.

A short trans man with a light-colored mustache and visible chest hair greeted us.

"Hey," said Dan's girlfriend to, presumably, her room-mate. For once, she did not sound as though she cared about another's perception of her. Maybe she was preoccupied with her errand.

She led me past a damp-smelling open bathroom and into her room. "We're here."

She turned on a switch, causing bright-blue light to stream down from the ceiling. A two-person bed took up almost the entire room. I saw our reflections in the mirrored sliding closet door, obscured by the bed from the hips down. I automatically scanned my body and face for flaws. Provisionally, I looked okay, but the mirror was too close to provide a holistic image in the cramped space.

Dan's girlfriend's bed and floor were covered with clothes. A single garment lay neatly on the unmade bed, apart from the other items. It was a large black turtleneck sweater. Dan's girlfriend picked up the sweater.

"So Dan wants me to wear this for the book club."

"Wait – is that why we came all the way over here?" I asked.

Dan's girlfriend posed with the sweater in front of her. "He thinks it will heighten the impact of your presentation if I wear this."

She arched her back in an exaggerated way.

"He's teaching me how to dress like an intellectual. It's very hot," she assured me.

"I see."

I looked at Dan's girlfriend holding the sweater. The fabric was shiny in the harsh light. The wool looked thick, yet slightly uncomfortable. I could definitely imagine her wearing it, how she'd look. I could easily envision the appearance he was trying to make her assume.

"It is hot," I agreed. "I can imagine wearing that as a woman."

Without answering me, Dan's girlfriend began to rifle through the contents of a large suitcase. She picked up and put down a series of undergarments.

"It's so tiring sometimes, being the hot girlfriend," she said.

"Yeah, I bet," I said sarcastically.

"Sorry for the mess, by the way. I don't really care about it. I don't spend any time here," she divulged.

"No. Dan's place is definitely better," I agreed.

I glanced at my reflection in the closet door — frowning, contrasting harshly against the white walls. Standing, yet again, on the periphery of someone's room, with that fake, neutral expression. I suddenly disliked how I looked.

I turned my attention back to Dan's girlfriend.

"What's wrong with your current outfit?" I asked.

She had taken off her jacket and was wearing a white, fitted tank top underneath. I could see a faded tattoo on her upper arm.

"I mean, its still kind of feminine and oppressive. You look like the girls who were popular in my middle school, haha."

Dan's girlfriend held up a lacy woman's undergarment. She appeared to contemplate it.

"You know what, no," she said finally.

"What do you mean? It's a very conformist look. Very attractive— "

"I'm gonna get something else. Wait here."

5

I sat on Dan's girlfriend's bed for some time. I looked in the closet door mirror, balancing on the edge of the unstable mattress. Maybe my face looked fine, I thought. I had my speech prepared for the book club. I looked over the notes on my phone. I would speak out against cities' over-reliance on tax credits and other forms of support that necessitate partnerships between governments and private developers. I would speak out against neoliberalism.

I picked up part of the black sweater, which Dan's girl-friend had thrown across the bed. As I had predicted, the fabric was soft yet slightly uncomfortable to the touch. I checked my email on my phone. I decided to send F.F. a separate email, in addition to Dan's girlfriend's message.

I heard footsteps. For some reason, even as I meditated on the wording of my email, I kept touching the sweater. Was Dan really making his girlfriend wear it?

It was immaterial, of course, to my life, but I really did have sexual fantasies about being a woman with a man. I imagined such a woman, who was and wasn't me, wearing an uncomfortable sweater. The fantasies were about being constrained, in every part of my life, in and out of the sex encounter, by imagined social norms for women. Being imprisoned in my body, unable to act or make choices in a life that was not my own – and then the frantic agitation of such a life, directed towards its only permissible outlet. And of course the man would only be a bland (or sometimes tragic) manifestation of those other norms, the masculine ones.

Even now – even though they had no place in my actual trysts with men – these were the only sexual fantasies I had.

Dan's girlfriend strode into the room as I was considering the implications of this fact. She climbed onto the bed.

"Okay, turn around," she told me.

"What?" I dropped the sweater.

"Or, actually, you don't have to turn around if you don't want to. I don't think breasts are necessarily sexual."

I quickly turned away.

"Look," she commanded.

I looked again. She now wore a mid-length binder for trans men. It was black, and compressed most of her upper chest area.

"I got this from my roommate," she said.

She turned to look at her flattened chest. I looked at her. She was no longer wearing glasses. I could immediately tell she would also have been conventionally attractive as a gay man.

"Um, what are you supposed to be wearing?"

"I'm a guy!" she shouted, in a slightly shrill tone.

She jumped up and began rummaging in the closet.

She put on a baseball cap. She put it on backwards, then forwards. She pulled her hair back and put it through the hole at the back of the hat. She put on a black tank top over the binder, with cut-off sleeves, such that parts of the binder were visible through the armholes.

She posed, holding an undersized bicep in front of the mirror.

"Don't I make a great trans guy?"

I saw that the tattoo on her upper arm was the Triforce triangle from *Zelda*, crudely rendered in yellow and washed-out blue – presumably from a time before she was Dan's girlfriend.

"My name can be Link. No, Eliott!" she decided.

I looked at her. It was true that her somewhat transformed appearance – the self-aware, asymmetrical grin, the baseball cap (which, in fact, bore a Yankees logo), the exposed, superficially wholesome, tomboyish, youthful features – triggered a familiar disdain.

"I thought I was the one who was supposedly 'transphobic.'"

"I'm not being transphobic!" she shouted, with the same raucous affect.

She started throwing clothes on the bed. She seemed to have come to some sort of decision about Dan, and was now behaving in an impulsive, chaotic manner. I tried to redirect the frustration I now felt.

"So you're going to the book club like this?"

"I just think it would be really funny."

"I guess."

I checked the time. It was 7:45.

"Because all these queer activist spaces always prioritize the voices of masculine people and specifically trans men," she said. "So it would be really funny if I went to the book club and everyone thought I was a trans guy!"

"Oh, okay."

She suddenly turned serious. "You know, I would actually kill to be in F.'s book club. I would literally kill. But I'm only getting to go to it because of you."

"Okay," I repeated. "Well, we should go now."

Dan's girlfriend made a final performance in front of the mirror. She frowned experimentally and adjusted her baseball cap brim so that it faced up, then down. She brushed past me as she walked towards the door.

"So, let's go?" she said. She looked at me, waiting.

I looked at her. I considered, again, her face, her voice, her gestures. Even now, even as she was being ostensibly mocking or sarcastic or impatient, she kept scanning my face for signs of what I was thinking. I found myself trying to reconcile the many contradictory impressions that her current appearance evoked.

"Okay," I said finally. "If you're going to do this, then I have to do one thing."

Dan's girlfriend laughed.

"There's no time," she urged.

"There is time," I said. "It will be a quick thing."

She looked exactly like a frenzied, overwrought woman dressed like a man. She looked exactly like a trans man, one who was overly comfortable using the signifiers of mainstream "queer" culture, and was therefore – also a feminine trait – probably secretly conformist. And she looked exactly like my childhood fantasy of what being a gay man would be like, the imagined freedom of that, so different from the reality. The shape of her mouth especially suggested this, wide and turned up at the corners. Even Dan probably wouldn't get why that was attractive.

"I am dressing up as a woman. And I know what my trans woman name would be," I said. I was suddenly inspired. "I know the perfect mythological name."

I paused.

"It's Cassandra," I said. "Because then no one would listen to me," I explained. "In case you don't get it."

☞

At first, Dan's girlfriend did not accede to my proposition. But it was too late. The didactic yet thoughtless way in which she protested the supposed untimeliness of my request – as if she had not already caused our delay, as if she were not, in fact, more interested in fulfilling her emotional needs, foreboding hole that they were, than in the successful execu‿

tion of any actual plan — only made me more determined to make my point. I launched into an explanation of why I needed to wear borrowed feminine clothes to the book club. I mentioned, again, my view of gender roles, the various social pressures facing men and women, the role of trans people.

"Being able to dress up as a woman as a joke is actually the pinnacle of masculinity," I said. "Objectifying your body and having it not matter, because everyone inherently believes you have agency— "

"Fine, just put this on," said Dan's girlfriend

She picked up a red dress off the closet floor. It had short puffy sleeves and ruffles.

"The shoulders are too wide," I said. "It's too fetishistic, not actually oppressive."

"Oh my god," said Dan's girlfriend.

"I am not wearing this," I insisted. "You probably wore this to, like, a sex party."

Dan's girlfriend looked at me appraisingly. She looked as if she was about to say something, but didn't. I realized she was assessing my physical appearance.

"Can't I wear something classier?" I asked.

I looked up "black funeral dress" on my phone, and showed her the results.

"I don't have anything like that," said Dan's girlfriend.

"Are you sure?"

"You're not going to a funeral!"

"Right, okay."

I suddenly became aware of the reality of my proposed actions. I had tried cross-dressing publicly once before, at the tech bootcamp (I had wanted to impress my then-colleagues at a Halloween party), but for whatever reason I had quickly changed back. I wondered if it would be different this time. I stood next to the bed.

"Are you going to put on the dress?" asked Dan's girlfriend.

"Yes! Maybe I'll wear something over it for modesty – like that sweater Dan wanted you to wear."

The desire to show what I needed to show to Dan's girlfriend now superseded – or rather began to seem like a prerequisite to – whatever else I hoped to achieve in the future.

"Then do it," she urged.

I straightened my already upright posture. "What? Don't tell me what to do."

She leaned closer to me. "Don't be smart with me, Cassie," she said in my ear.

I straightened my posture so much that I almost fell backwards. Her words and physical proximity were genuinely disorienting, which meant the argument I was trying to make was working.

"Fine," I said. "Okay. No one listens to Cassandra."

I ended up putting on the dress. It had an open back, with big ribbons stretching across the opening. Dan's girlfriend secured them for me one by one, adjusting the large decorative bows, making each one slightly tighter than necessary. I thought about a man – someone like Dan, perhaps, but no, perhaps not necessarily him – an oppressed man making a woman wear a dress, taking pleasure in the woman's oppression.

Dan's girlfriend stepped back. "Let me get this straight. You're planning to change back when you do the speech?" she asked.

"Yes," I said.

I was still slightly dazed from the experience of her assistance with the garment.

"Otherwise – isn't being a generic conservative bro, like, your whole brand?"

I looked down. The bottom of the dress went down to mid-thigh. Below, I could see my legs, bruised and misshapen from childhood soccer injuries and weightlifting.

"Yes, obviously," I said.

I moved my feet closer together, vaguely embarrassed by my black socks, practical garments I had purchased in bulk online.

"I guess there's not time to shave my legs," I observed.

Dan's girlfriend's gaze, again, lingered on my person. She looked down at my exposed thighs.

"I have tights you can use."

"Uh, okay, cool."

Dan's girlfriend entered the closet and began to rummage in one of the suitcases. I looked, again, in the closet door mirror. The bed was blocking my view of my lower body. However, the upper portion of my body looked almost equally undignified – the face, especially, with its serious expression, superimposed over the unflattering wide, square neck opening of the dress. Perhaps, I told myself, I looked normal. From many angles, I told myself, I merely looked like a conventional drag performer.

"Try these on," said Dan's girlfriend, giving me a pair of crumpled tights.

I quickly took off my socks and put on the tights, jamming my legs into the narrow openings. Yet this did not diminish the all too familiar sensation of unwanted bodily vulnerability. I felt my thighs touching. I saw many individual large hairs pressed down by the translucent, flesh-colored fabric. I sat down on the bed.

"These have a hole in them," I told Dan's girlfriend. I sounded more upset than I had intended.

She sat down next to me. I felt our bodies collide on the sagging mattress.

"You're right," she said. She ran her hand along the long line of torn fabric. "Well, we can fix that."

Dan's girlfriend stood up. Then she left the room. I continued to look in the mirror at my exposed upper chest and back. When she came back, the trans man with the mustache was with her. He looked at me with critical curiosity. He leaned back in an exaggerated way. It was her roommate.

"Looking good!" he said.

"Haha, thanks!"

I looked in the mirror. I observed my trapezius muscle, which sloped up visibly through the wide neck opening.

"I really love the ruffles," said the roommate. "Very magical girl. Very whimsical."

"Thank you," I repeated, with a presumably more feminine intonation.

I continued to look in the mirror. The open neck and exposed trapezius ironically made my shoulders look overly narrow, clashing with the masculine secondary sex characteristics I still possessed. My back, on the other hand, looked acceptable, or at least legible – encased by red ribbons, it bore the stylized, conventionally yielding look of theatrically "oppressed" flesh. Maybe if everything stayed like this, if my perceptions stayed fixed to that one, relatively innocuous glimpse of my back, I could almost proceed normally and feel fine. I could now see why I had changed out of my "costume" almost immediately at the tech boot camp.

"Okay, we need your help," Dan's girlfriend interrupted my thoughts. She was addressing the roommate.

"Let's go to my room," he said, grimacing at the fluorescent ceiling light. "The lighting here isn't doing us any favors."

We went to his room. The roommate's room was bigger than Dan's girlfriend's room, and did seem to have dimmer, yellower light, which came from strings of bulbs on the walls and ceiling. It illuminated an orderly, domestic space – a window with burnt-orange curtains, a bed with purple sheets, a row of standing mannequin torsos by the wall, one of which wore a pink bra over its sculpted pectoral muscles. An oval-shaped full-length mirror stood in the corner.

"So, I have a whole bunch of stockings you can wear," said the roommate, opening a large wardrobe. He dumped a collection of hosiery on the bed. "Stockings are such a confidence boost," he went on.

He began to narrate as he held up individual pairs of lacy black and brown garments. "I love wearing a pair of stockings in a crowd. And its actually more practical than people think. You need to get a high-quality, comfortable belt with solid enclosures in the back. Elastic suspenders. Don't get the plastic clips. I know some independent boutiques where you can get vintage-style belts with metal clasps, which have six or eight straps. That's three or four straps per leg," he said.

"We're in a hurry bro. Just give her something sexy to wear," said Dan's girlfriend.

She looked at my bare legs and upper chest. In the hat, she looked like a caricature of a man.

"Something for a night out," she said.

"An intellectual night out," I said. My voice sounded like it was coming from another person. "At a book club."

Dan's girlfriend kept looking at me, until I finally looked away.

"But no, I think I'm gonna put my normal clothes in a bag. I think I will change back when I do the speech," I said.

Dan's girlfriend nodded. "I respect that. She's got a primary to win," she explained to the roommate.

"Mhm," said the latter.

"She's gonna be America's first transgender congressman. Or was it the third transgender congressman?" she asked.

"Well, I would be the third official candidate from a major political party who is trans," I said, pushing down the folds of the dress. "And there are currently some trans women serving in state legislatures. But I would be the first trans person serving in the US Congress, if I am elected."

"There you go," she told the roommate.

"Cool, cool," said the roommate. He began to arrange the stockings on the bed into piles. "I know a lot of people who worked on campaigns. Just remember, if you do any kind of data entry or phone banking, its time-consuming work and it takes a lot more out of you than you think. You want to budget at least half a day of recovery for each day that you do it, and you want to make a big lunch," he advised. "You can also eat nuts throughout the day, which keeps your blood sugar levels normal. Almonds and cashews. Especially if you tend to have low blood sugar, which a lot of people do."

I nodded vigorously. "I'll keep that in mind for my staffers," I told him.

Finally, the roommate found a set of beige stockings and matching garter belt I could wear. I put the stockings on carefully this time, stepping into the openings in my bare feet. I maneuvered the belt under the red dress. When I had adjusted everything, it fit snugly around my waist, and the stockings stayed secure on my upper thighs. Dan's girlfriend stood next to me in front of the mirror. I could not see the tops of the stockings under the bottom of the dress, but I could feel them encasing my thighs, right below the elastic leg openings of my boxer briefs. Dan's girlfriend put her arm around my waist. She was almost as tall as me, but I was not wearing shoes.

Dan's girlfriend held out her phone. "What do you think? We look like a fucking hot pair of transsexuals!" she said.

I looked at our images on the screen. With her single strand of blond hair emerging from beneath the baseball cap and mischievous, slightly upturned grin, she really did look like a grinning, harmless trans guy, at least on camera. My face looked incoherent again. I mentally blocked it from my view.

"We *definitely* do," I said.

"Mhm," said the roommate again, nodding indulgently. He began to list the names of queer and trans venues and events. "So are you going anywhere in particular?"

Dan's girlfriend shook her head. "We're just going to the book club," she said. "And then we are going home."

"Yes," I agreed.

Dan's girlfriend took a picture.

We did not end up going to the book club. Dan's girlfriend put my regular clothes and phone into a reusable shopping bag, which she chivalrously held in her hand as we got on the train. The overhead train rumbled and screeched in the dark. It was, I realized, around 8:15. Despite our attempts to expedite our cross-dressing, we were running extremely late. Dan's girlfriend was about to send F.F. a new series of messages, which were to include a fictitious excuse about the train, when she got another text message from Dan.

"Don't communicate with F. anymore," he instructed. "Do not send her more texts. There is too much going on tonight, and she's already overwhelmed."

I leaned on Dan's girlfriend's shoulder, which seemed appropriate given our current presentations. I looked at her phone.

"I honestly don't think Ashton should go there tonight," Dan had written. "Housing policy is a complex topic, and I don't think he's ready."

"What?" I exclaimed. Several people looked up. It was no longer rush hour, but the train was still crowded. "I've done nothing but read about housing policy!"

"Shh," said Dan's girlfriend. She opened another incoming message.

"It makes much more sense for him to go next month," it said. "That would be great timing actually, with F.'s article coming out in June. Let's regroup Monday to kick things off officially."

The message ended with a smiley face. I leaned closer, trying to catch a glimpse of what else Dan had written, but Dan's girlfriend quickly put the phone away. She put her arm around me, propping up my body in its leaning position.

I looked around to see if anyone on the train had noticed, but it seemed that no one had. Across from us, a group of women were looking at each other's phones.

"He's saying we shouldn't go to the book club?" I asked.

I tried to make it sound like I still wanted to go. On some level I did, but I also didn't. Dan's girlfriend repositioned my head on her shoulder.

"You saw the text."

"I thought she really doesn't like it when people cancel last-minute."

"She doesn't like it," said Dan's girlfriend.

"'Better to come late than not at all,'" I said, quoting from one of her better-known books, *The Principles of Collective Organizing*.

Dan's girlfriend withdrew from me slightly.

"You could go by yourself if you wanted!"

"Um," I said.

I looked at my feet, encased in their borrowed, pointed-toed block heel shoes. It was hard to think. She drew closer to me, relenting.

"I think that she and Dan are talking to each other again," she said. "I've seen him do this before. Some version of it."

"Oh, okay," I said. "I guess that's good?"

"It's fine. They've probably been texting each other nonstop."

I put my head under her chin. I looked at our transparent reflections in the train window, our contrasting hairstyles and clothes. Normally, I would have felt inspired or agitated by this disclosure about Dan, this revelation of lots of secret activity on his part, but what he was doing seemed remote from what was now happening. "So they are friends now?" I said.

"Straight men are incapable of friendship."

"Oh, okay."

As she spoke, I continued to observe my face in the train window. Did it now look better? Cross-dressing definitely was not comfortable, I reflected. Yet it now also felt natural to put my innate discomfort on display in this manner. And actually, I realized, I had had a similar motivation when I initially told Dan that I would run for Congress – that I "might as well" put my so-called lack of a comfort zone, my willingness to do anything for the right kind of attention, to use for some greater good. I wondered what "greater good" I was trying to achieve now.

Dan's girlfriend interrupted my thoughts by throwing her body over me in a violent, protective embrace.

"What's wrong?" I asked.

"Keep your head down. Those women are trying to take a picture of you," she whispered loudly.

"Wow, really?"

She pushed the top of my head down. "Yes," she said. "It's happened to me a bunch of times. And don't yell."

I glanced up at the women sitting across from us – the same ones that had been looking at each other's phones earlier. One of them now, indeed, held her phone pointed in our direction. I lifted my head up slightly and smiled at the women.

Maybe I had that in common with Dan's girlfriend, I thought. Maybe that need for attention, which I had initially found so objectionable, was actually what I had in common with her. In fact, I knew it to be true. That was probably why, earlier, she had reminded me of my childhood fantasy of "being a gay man."

I had fantasized about that kind of "gay male relationship," no doubt, as a child or isolated teen, raised on naive, female-written media about male friendship – a relationship where each party recognized in the other that need for attention, and emotionally supported each other in that knowledge – the freedom and imagined relief that would come from that.

I looked at the women. I allowed Dan's girlfriend's sprawled form to protect me from their gaze. Would it really be so bad if they took a picture of me? I thought of the picture Dan's girlfriend had taken of me earlier. I was moved to imagine her suffering, in the past, through a version of the vulnerability I now felt.

The train came to a stop.

"Oh, that reminds me," I said. "Could you maybe not post the pictures you took of me on social media? They can be for your private collection."

But Dan's girlfriend just grabbed my hand. With her other hand, she picked up the shopping bag filled with my clothes. The women were now definitely looking at us.

"Let's just get off the train here," said Dan's girlfriend.

We strode past the three women.

"I think you're beautiful," said the one who had supposedly been taking a picture of me as we walked past.

꒦

Dan's girlfriend and I stood on the empty train platform, surrounded by the silhouettes of housing projects and office buildings. The lights of the bridge blinked in the distance.

"I guess we're not going to the book club?"

Dan's girlfriend turned towards the exit. A gust of cold wind swept over the platform, from which the open-back dress I was wearing offered little protection. I huddled against Dan's girlfriend for warmth.

"No," she agreed. "If we go now, it will just stress out Dan."

She wrapped her arm around me to protect me from the wind Purple clouds moved overhead. I felt the ribbons in the back of my dress flutter in the breeze. I realized that the Parking Lot, the gay bar where I had initially encountered Dan's girlfriend, was only a few blocks away from this station.

"We could go to the Parking Lot," I suggested.

Dan's girlfriend seemed pleased with this proposition.

"That's an idea! I've never been there on a Friday night."

"It's probably a lot of fun," I told her.

She walked ahead of me. I followed her into the street.

We went towards the bar. I navigated the sidewalks carefully as we walked through Williamsburg, trying not to fall or seem off-balance in my chunky heels. We walked past a series of condominiums, a garage, an intersection where several men leered at us.

"You're getting better at walking in heels," Dan's girlfriend remarked.

"Thanks."

We had our arms around each other's waists. We really were a pair of "hot transsexuals" enjoying the city's famous nightlife. It was almost better than being seen as a conventional heterosexual couple. Dan's girlfriend offered me a cigarette, and I took it.

"I guess I'm taking this joke to its logical conclusion!" I declaimed.

"I do like that about you," she answered. "Your *consistent* willingness to commit to the bit."

I blew out a large puff of smoke. "What a trivializing expression," I said. I bent down to look her in the eye. I was about two inches taller than her, now, in my heels. "Nothing about my life is a 'bit'," I asserted.

Dan's girlfriend gaped at me. "Okay, sure." She made air quotes. "'Cassandra'."

We arrived at the bar shortly after this exchange. We turned a corner, and I saw the familiar panorama — the chain-link fence, the red door, the line of orange cones from a nearby construction site. I recalled the feelings of social anxiety and vague hope normally evoked by this scenery — unworthy remnants of a former life.

There were more people standing outside than usual. I threw away my cigarette. As a civic-minded aspiring party primary nominee, I would normally have put it in my pocket to avoid littering, but the dress had no pockets.

"We should go in," I said. "It looks like a real party!"

"Is everyone here straight?" said Dan's girlfriend.

"I think its the weekly eighties-themed dance night," I confirmed.

"That is hilariously lame," said Dan's girlfriend, "let's go inside!"

She looked at me. "I normally don't like saying 'lame' as a pejorative term," she added.

She led me inside. In the cramped entryway, the man who guarded the door scowled at us while she searched the reusable shopping bag for my wallet. While I was waiting for her to find the wallet, a man and woman from outside the bar approached me.

"You're beautiful," said the woman. She spoke with a significantly more drunk affect than the woman on the train.

"Aw, thanks," I said.

And I meant it. My appearance was the cathartic outward expression of what was normally hidden in my relations with others — that desperate, shamefully feminine need for attention — for validation — which I had perceived and judged so harshly in Dan's girlfriend. A look best reserved for special occasions, which this was.

I smiled graciously at the woman.

"You should be free to express yourself," she shouted at me, leaning unsteadily against her companion.

Dan's girlfriend thrust my wallet into my hand.

"I will be," I answered.

We went further into the bar. Inside, it was too loud to talk. A version of a well-known eighties pop song was playing, loudly, and a mass of shuffling, gyrating people occupied the entire indoor seating area and stage. Cologne, deodorant, and body odor mingled with and almost supplanted the underlying scent of cleaning product. Patrons repeatedly collided with each other in the hallway.

Dan's girlfriend pressed up against me in the crush of people. "How long do you actually want to stay here?" she asked.

I looked around. There were far too many people in front of the bar.

"Maybe we can dance," I shouted.

"I'm down."

Dan's girlfriend grabbed my hand and led me into the middle of the roiling mass. I started dancing next to her, moving my body from side to side, careful not to tip over as I put weight on the balls of my feet. I moved closer to her. I felt the various parts of my outfit constraining me as I shuffled back and forth, more or less in time to the eighties music. It was actually not hard to imagine myself as a woman. I let myself become absorbed in the rhythmic, cloying, slightly distorted sounds.

"You are the hottest guy I ever saw – Link," I said.

Dan's girlfriend pushed me up against a pool table. I sat on the edge of the pool table. She was eye level with me. I don't know why I keep calling her Dan's girlfriend. Her actual name was Lilliana or Thalia or something like that. Dan's girlfriend grasped me by the shoulders and moved her face very close to mine. Then she suddenly turned away.

"I'll buy you a drink," she said.

I looked up, dazed. "That would be cool, yeah," I acquiesced.

Dan's girlfriend led me through the vast throng surrounding the bar. The bartender, a brisk, unfamiliar man in a black metal T-shirt, instinctively turned to her. She ordered two vodka sodas.

"Now you owe me for next time."

"Okay," I said.

The crowd surged around me. I briefly wondered what she meant by "next time." Suddenly, I felt someone tug on one of my puffy sleeves. I turned around.

I saw a man in a flat-brimmed baseball cap, with a defined jaw. He had prominent bones around the mouth, a look I used to strive to emulate sometimes when posing for photos. The white Yankees logo on his baseball cap looked red under the flickering lights. It was the man from the train — the man who had asked us about this bar. He now sat at the bar, seemingly alone, with a drink.

"Just wanted to express my appreciation, uh, for helping me find this place!" he shouted.

"Haha, thanks," I said.

The man reached out towards me again. He touched my sleeve. His hand lingered on the crinkly polyester fabric.

"Uh," I said.

I looked around for Dan's girlfriend. She had not moved far. She was still there on the other side of me, but was now seated at the bar. She had found an unoccupied seat. She had our two drinks in front of her, and had her phone out. She was, again, quickly typing into it.

I closed the distance between me and Dan's girlfriend, so that the man could see that we were together — an echo or inversion of my earlier, masculine gesture on the train. I wondered what a woman would do in this situation. I took one of the drinks, and drained its contents.

"Uh, maybe you could buy me a second drink?" I asked the man.

The man stared at me. He said something inaudible.

"What?" I asked.

"Sure!" he shouted. He fumbled with my sleeve again. He started to take out his wallet.

I looked away suggestively, then looked back at the man. I could not tell if he saw.

"Thank you!" I said.

Dan's girlfriend was ignoring me. I continued to stand between her and the man.

"How is your night going?!" he shouted in my ear.

I felt his hand on my shoulder. I put my lips close to the man's ear and was about to shout, "Fine!" I turned and saw Dan's girlfriend staring at both of us. She was no longer on her phone. She and the man were both wearing Yankees caps, I noted, but hers looked more transmasculine and ironic.

"What are you doing?" she asked. I could not tell which one of us she was addressing, but it did not matter. Her face bore its now-familiar expression of exaggerated, impatient concern.

"Do you want to keep talking to this person?" she asked me.

She was really perceiving me, I thought. It was not just her own theatrics. She knew me.

"Uh, not really," I said, embarrassed.

"Okay."

She took my hand. She pocketed her phone and got up, leaving behind the remaining, partially consumed drink. I followed her, past the bar, into the narrow hallway to one side of the stage, by the bathrooms. It still smelled like bleach-based cleaning products. Dan's girlfriend stopped. She pushed me against a wall. I stared at her.

"Thank you for indulging me," she said.

"Yes, of course," I said. I felt a pleasurable embarrassment. "You mean now, or — earlier?"

Dan's girlfriend moved closer. Several loud bar patrons walked by.

"Dan texted me saying I shouldn't come over tonight," she told me.

I pressed myself further against the wall. I felt its slightly sticky surface against my bare back — its comforting verticality.

"Uh, were you planning to?" I asked.

Dan's girlfriend did not answer. Someone turned on the dryer fan in one of the bathrooms.

"Well, I live alone now, so," I said eventually.

This was true. I had actually moved out of my old place, with its three roommates, months ago, after soliciting Dan's advice.

"So you could come over if you want," I finished my sentence.

Dan's girlfriend still did not say anything. She opened one of the bathroom doors. With a sense of inevitability, I followed her inside. The cleaning product smell got stronger.

"Excuse me," she said to a departing patron.

When we were alone, she directed me into the bathroom's solitary stall. The dryer fan turned on again, then turned off. The stall door did not have a working lock and kept swinging open. She motioned for me to sit on top of the toilet tank. I obeyed her.

"We're gonna have sex in this dirty bathroom stall," she informed me.

"Okay," I said.

I tried to prepare myself for what that would entail. I put my feet on the toilet seat. I put my back up against the wall. Dan's girlfriend grabbed the toilet plunger in the corner of the stall. I thought she intended to penetrate me with it during the sex act, but no. She jammed the plunger inside the stall door crevice, causing it to stay open at a forty five-degree angle. This, in turn, impeded the main bathroom door from opening, blocking all outside access into the bathroom.

When she was done with this task, she turned and faced me across the toilet seat. She became serious.

"Well," she said.

She leaned across the toilet seat and kissed me on the lips. It did not initially feel like I had imagined.

This whole time – at the bar, on the train, outside the restaurant, or when I hung out with Dan, or even before that, when I was a child or teen or naive adolescent – I had been fantasizing about what it would feel like, this final, definitive moment of relief with someone like this, a person "like me" whom I understood, and perhaps opposed, and possibly also admired – a transformative moment of mutual communion or recognition or confession. This encounter, at first, did not feel like that.

I continued to make out with Dan's girlfriend. I felt our tongues touching. She undid the top ribbon of my dress. She began to grope, fondle, and embrace various parts of my body. She worked with noticeably confident, practiced gestures, and made sure, at each step, to ask me for consent, something I had scoffed at in every previous sexual encounter I had.

When she started to take off my underwear, they became entangled in the straps attached to her roommate's high-quality, vintage-style stockings, which otherwise held up well under the strain of our activity. The sensation of twisting fabric and elastic, awkwardly bunching around areas of unexpected, excessive feminine fat distribution, was, of course, provocative and upsetting. Maybe it was that – merely that sensation, and not who she was as a person – which made me realize that, actually, I could do it. I could easily imagine myself as a woman. I could easily respond sexually to what was happening. Why hadn't I been able to do this before?

I saw her as my high school boyfriend. I saw her as a long-suffering man. Yes, even when she asked me for "consent" in that characteristic, nominal, moralizing way, it was easy to respond sexually. Hadn't my consent already been violated – long ago, yes, but also now?

It was appropriate that we were doing this in the bathroom, I thought vaguely. It was just like relieving yourself in public. An embarrassing yet all-too-possible physical act.

꒕

I did not reach a sexual climax while we were in the bathroom, but I felt sure that I could have, given enough time. Yet eventually, before that could have, perhaps, happened, after a period of aggressive knocking, a hand forced its way inside the bathroom door. It held a gray reusable shopping bag.

"Is this your bag?" asked the person on the other side of the door.

Their forearm was covered with abstract, geometric tattoos. It was the bartender from the bar.

"Someone is looking for you," he said.

"Fuck," said Dan's girlfriend. "I'm sorry about this."

She pulled up her jeans.

"I didn't tell him where we were. He must have called someone," she told me. She took the bag out of the bartender's disembodied, proffered hand and looked through it.

She meant Dan.

Dan's Girlfriend grabbed the black wool sweater from inside the bag. It had been there the whole time — she must have put it there, the turtleneck sweater Dan had wanted her to wear to the book club. She quickly put on the sweater, vigorously sticking her head through the tight neck opening. She gave me the hat she had been wearing. She gave me the bag.

I put down the hat and bag, untangled my boxer briefs from the eight elastic straps still affixed to the roommate's stockings and garter belt (four per leg), and then again picked up the hat and bag. I picked up my heels, which I had taken off while we were having sex.

We exited the bathroom. I heard the exuberant guitar chords of the song "Rio."

Dan's girlfriend pulled me aside.

"You know this doesn't change anything," she announced.

"Well..." I began to say. I was about to protest, to tell her that for me this changed a great deal.

She looked at me intently. "You still have every chance of getting elected."

"And you can help me with that!" I offered.

"No. Look at me," she insisted. "Dan has made me read all his books. I know all about the housing crisis."

"I've learned a lot— "

Her eyes bore into mine. She radiated telepathic waves of conviction.

"Everybody already knows," she said, "what the right policies are to solve the crisis. It's not a question of *knowing*" – she emphasized the word – "which policies to pursue."

What she was saying was true, I reflected. I had already been nominated. Maybe, even if she wanted to, and in spite of my non-appearance at the book club, F.F. wouldn't be able to rescind the nomination. But I was still in love with her.

"You're probably right," I said.

"Of course I'm right," said Dan's girlfriend. She assumed a brisk, cheerful affect. "I'm gonna be New York's first female mayor."

"Is that so?" I said stiffly.

Dan's girlfriend touched my cheek. She made, perhaps, some other affectionate gesture. But that was it. I was engaging with her as Cassandra for the last time.

"Maybe I'll run against you," I said nonsensically. "Maybe I'll be New York's first female mayor!"

She laughed. We went to find Dan. When we did, I tried to warn him about emotions, but he would not listen.

PORN

"Lex" woke up on the floor. Her mouth was dry, her boxer briefs felt crusty and gross. She was still wearing her sweatshirt, and about five layers of clothing under that. She had been awakened by the heat, but also by the stench of her own body. The carpet was brown. The room was dim. The window had venetian blinds, but she could see through the slats that it was reasonably late in the day. Next to her was a backpack, a bus schedule, a copy of *The Confessions* of Jean-Jacques Rousseau that she had been trying to read, and a porn magazine with instructions for making burritos written on the back.

It was the house from the party she had gone to yesterday. She had smoked marijuana and fallen asleep on the floor. She heard activity in the kitchen. She wondered if she could get to the bathroom without being seen by whoever it was.

Wrestling with her unconscious will to death, she got up. This allowed her to see over the counter. Sure enough, there was a man, a dude, in the kitchen. He faced away from her. He appeared to be putting dishes away – except for the ones that had food remnants on them, which he left alone. The digital clock on the microwave said it was almost three.

There was no getting past this man unseen.

"Hey, uh, good morning or something," said Lex.

The man, or dude, turned around. He was just a late-twenties guy with brown hair and a beard.

"Hey there," said Lex. "I was gonna ask if there was a bathroom here I could use, but I guess I don't need to, right?"

The man picked at his beard, but didn't answer.

"I'd better get going if I'm gonna start looking for a job today. I got fired from my old job like a month ago," she explained.

"Huh? Just do what you want," he said.

"Sure," said Lex, flustered.

Lex decided he actually had nice classical European features under that stupid beard. A lot of people did. Maybe that's what Rousseau looked like, she thought, except with no beard and a wig probably.

Lex wondered about what other people were like. Lex was the kind of person who contemplated other people's personalities the way a layperson might (after, perhaps, reading a short article on physics or astrology) be moved to wonder about the stars.

The bearded individual went back to his kitchen tasks.

"Well, then I'm off," Lex said, giving up on the possibility of the bathroom.

She put the bus schedule and the copy of *Confessions* into her backpack. She looked at the porn magazine. With bemused dismay, she remembered the events of last night.

T5

At a certain point in the evening, she recalled, they'd gone to either Matt's or Eric's room to smoke marijuana. Among the assorted items on the floor – cigarette packs and various event flyers – Lex's eye had been drawn instinctively (as would anyone's, she thought) to the bright lurid cover with the unreadable name, obscured by two topless women with prominent, shiny, gumdrop-shaped breasts that leapt right off the page, into the viewer's face. It was *Club* magazine. Whoever's room this was had two or three issues lying around.

"Hey, look at that!" Lex had said, after clearing a place for herself close to the door. She picked up one of the issues of *Club*.

Lex looked at Jennifer. Jennifer had cleared a place for herself next to the bed, not far from Lex. Jennifer was a full-figured young woman in a hooded sweatshirt and shorts. She had long red hair and pale skin that looked like it had lotion applied to it regularly. Eric was some guy who lived here.

"My god, just look at this incredible artifact!" Lex continued excitedly. She was encouraged by the look of lively interest in Jennifer's eyes, directed at her. Lex pointed at the two thong-clad models on the cover.

"Ha, ha," said Jennifer.

"Heh, heh," said Matt's girlfriend, Katie or something.

Matt's girlfriend, whom Lex did not like, was sitting below the bed, getting a massage from Matt. Matt was the younger manager of the coffee shop where Lex used to work, as of last month (he was not the manager who fired her; he was cool).

"Do you think that girl looks like you?" Eric asked Jennifer. He gestured at the lewd publication with a sinewy arm.

"Uh, which one?" asked Jennifer.

"Both of them. Hahaha," laughed Eric.

"Gross!" said Jennifer.

Lex found her nervous laughter attractive. She sounded desperate, like she was trying to help her interlocutor, even though he had perhaps insulted her. Jennifer reached out to Eric for the pipe. Matt continued to silently massage his girlfriend.

Lex struggled to express what she had meant about the porn magazine. "No! Well, I mean – yes – maybe they do kind of look like her," she admitted, "they both have red hair. But really the reason for the similarity is that her appearance *actually has the same degree of unreality as this image*. I mean, I used to think porn was so forbidden and exciting, but now? Well, let me tell you, I'm a pretty decent judge of female sexual attractiveness" – she looked at Jennifer again – "but I find this image to be pretty much the opposite of sexual, just because of how stridently it *refers* to sex. Maybe that's why I find porn so fascinating, artistically – precisely *because* of its remoteness from physical desire! Contemporary porn is platonic, ascetic – pure."

"Ugh, I know what you mean," said Jennifer. "Does *anyone* find these women attractive?"

She looked at Eric. Eric leaned back in his office chair, exhaling lustily. He gestured towards Matt and his girlfriend. Jennifer took a quick drag from the pipe and passed it to them.

"I don't think its about the women," said Matt. "It's more about, hm – lusting after something that's idealized. Like there's no messy preparation or anything. The sex is right there."

"Preparation?" asked Eric, raising an eyebrow.

"Like messing with their clothes and stuff," Matt said quickly. "Or peeing afterwards. For the woman."

"Hey!" said the girlfriend.

"Sorry," said Matt.

She meant the pipe. Matt maneuvered the glass implement into her waiting, partially open mouth and let her inhale. She coughed contentedly.

"I don't agree," said Eric, when Matt's girlfriend finished coughing. "I used to look at porn all the time. What can I say? I was a deprived young man."

Everyone laughed.

"I feel bad for you?" said Jennifer cautiously.

"Then I found out most porn can't even fucking begin to compare to the real thing," said Eric. "Fucking, that is." He looked to the others for agreement. "And note that I say 'fucking' to connote all sex acts," he added. "Like what is the alternative terminology? 'Making love'?"

"That sounds like something from a bad romance novel," agreed Matt's girlfriend, coughing again.

Eric shook his head.

"Fucking is dirty," he said. "But its a good dirty. It's earthy. It's not degrading. That's what people who don't really enjoy – well, fucking – don't understand."

"Fucking," said Matt's girlfriend, smiling lewdly.

"Fucking," said Jennifer, also smiling, but more thoughtfully.

Lex watched Jennifer look thoughtfully at Eric. It made Lex think of a billboard she used to see all the time in Los Angeles, when she rode the bus to downtown Los Angeles and back every night to sit alone in the nightclub. The billboard was for the show *Law & Order*. Seeing it always made Lex wish she had a girlfriend – someone like Jennifer, perhaps, who had probably had family or emotional problems in the past but had gotten her act together, gone to college, and had gotten a good job. Someone who'd buy entire seasons of *Law & Order* for them to watch in a high-quality format, and would talk to Lex about how "addicted" she was to its hard-hitting, impartial accounts of hardworking city officials.

Now that was real pornography, Lex thought to herself, smiling slightly at this irony.

"Having sex," said Eric. "Okay. I am having sex, you are having sex, we are having sex," he said, imitating Lex by speaking in a monotone. "You like sex, right?" he asked Lex. "I thought you were a lesbian, not asexual."

"Come on, she's not asexual," said Matt.

"I'm like Rousseau," said Lex, embarrassed.

Jennifer looked at her. "A romantic," clarified Lex.

"Hm," said Eric. He motioned again for Jennifer to sit by his feet.

"Haha," Jennifer laughed politely at Lex's statement, and then complied with Eric's invitation. She moved to where he was sitting, crouching in a possibly cringing way that Lex, again, found attractive. Seated on the chair, Eric encircled Jennifer's form with his long legs. At the same time, Matt passed the pipe to Lex. She inhaled, and began to cough uncontrollably.

"Wow, this is some good weed," said Lex.

"Sure," acknowledged Matt's girlfriend.

The discussion went on like this, full of spirited exchanges on the topics of drug use and sex.

Soon, Lex found herself becoming distant from what was happening, partially due to the effects of the weed. Inwardly, she began to compare her situation to that of a brain-damaged servant, trying to impress his masters by cooking an elaborate meal whose preparation went far beyond his meager abilities to read, remember, and follow directions. She wondered what would happen if she actually cooked a meal for everyone right now. "Uh, is there a computer here I can use real quick?" she asked.

"Huh? Uh, what for?"

"I believe that I have 'the munchies'." Lex made quotation marks with her fingers. "I need to look up burrito recipes on the internet and prepare them right in your kitchen."

"Ha, ha – you don't need a recipe to make burritos."

However, Lex did. They let her use the computer and, after she finally got the internet connection to work, locating and resetting the apartment's router, she found a website of simple recipes for people under the influence of marijuana. The site boasted that all the meals it listed could be prepared within minutes "right in your dorm kitchen."

Using the back of the same issue of *Club* magazine that she still held in her hand, Lex wrote down the instructions for how to make vegetarian burritos. She wasn't a vegetarian, but she thought it would be easier. She went into the deserted kitchen. Most people were still drinking outside.

Many hours later, hours that included a trip to a nearby 7-Eleven, issue of *Club* in hand, Lex managed to create five or six enormous, more or less intact, perfectly edible burritos that contained beans, rice, vegetables, sour cream, and shredded cheddar cheese.

Feeling somewhat more coherent, and accomplished, Lex returned to the room with her burritos piled high on a plate. She opened the door. Matt and his girlfriend were gone. Eric and Jennifer were having sex on the bed with the lights still on. It looked sordid and realistic – not pure or ascetic at all. Maybe it resembled European, amateur porn. When she'd been talking about the abstractness and asceticism of contemporary porn, she had forgotten about the phenomenon of European porn.

Lex left the room. She went back into the abandoned living room and proceeded to eat one-fifth of a single burrito. Then she fell asleep on the floor, trying to summon the energy to discreetly masturbate to *Club*.

Now, the next day, as Lex was getting ready to leave, she debated whether or not to put the magazine into her backpack. Would the bearded dude in the kitchen notice if she just took it? She thought she could use these instructions for burritos, if nothing else. "If I could just take this, uh, porn mag with me," she said. When the dude seemed not to have heard her, she took it and walked out into the street.

5

She walked in the blinding sunlight, thinking about how she would make burritos for herself tonight. She thought maybe she could also stop by the laundromat on the way home, the one with the cheap *Galaga* machine. She started to walk, but when she emerged from the residential side street onto the vast, smog-covered plane of Burnet Road where it intersected with Romeria Drive, she came to a dead stop.

There was nothing but the blue sky above, pavement and stores below. That, and for some reason a field of dead grass across the road from her. Moreover, she didn't have the money for *Galaga* or burritos. She couldn't even take the bus. She'd spent it all at the 7-Eleven last night, on burrito ingredients.

Lex crossed part of Burnet Road. She stood on the median and thought about what she should do. She could walk home. She could go back to the house and ask for her partially eaten burritos back. She could reply to romantic classified ads. She could ask her parents for money.

Instead, she rolled up the sleeves of her sweatshirt. It was a hot, sunny day. To her surprise, she felt calm. She was no one's brain-damaged servant now. She wasn't going to do any of those things. She stared at the field of dead grass.

Suddenly, several groups of children poured out of a low building into the field. Lex realized that she was standing in front of a middle school, and that classes had just ended for the day.

There were many small clusters of fat, homely children in oversized white T-shirts and blue jeans. There were a couple of bigger groups of athletic, handsome children in black skater clothes (on the boys) and revealing tank tops (on the girls). The girls in tank tops moved like they were part of a good, busy world of homework and friends. The boys in skater clothes moved with such underlying energy and power in their perpetually flexed backs and slightly too-large limbs that it made Lex distracted with envy and desire – but only for a moment.

Lex thought about her own middle school days. They were terrible. She had gone by a different name. She didn't have her current personality – the relaxed, itinerant house party attendee. The only thing she had back then was the internet. Lex had learned how to make a web page. Even though it was just about her hobbies at the time (making web sites and reading), she had used it to solicit emails from older men that she could tell were interested in her, and with whom she would also sometimes chat over messaging programs.

Then the whole internet porn controversy came out and Lex's mom started monitoring her internet use. There'd been a huge fight. Lex remembered how badly she'd wanted to look at porn, how badly she wanted the knowledge that would have, for once, put her above her peers.

In middle school, Lex would have paid anything for porn. She would have paid anything for just one photograph or obscene story. It was depressing how little that stuff was worth to her now.

Suddenly, Lex struck her own forehead at the obviousness of the idea. She looked in her backpack. The issue of *Club* was still there. She took it out, ripping off the back cover with the burrito instructions. Soon, she'd have more than enough money for those burritos.

Lex sat on the median in the middle of Burnet Road and tore page after page from the magazine. She worked quickly yet carefully, trying not to tear into any images or text. When she was done, she had a sheaf of loose pornographic pages in her hand.

Across the road, the clusters of children had split up and moved closer, as though cooperating with her plan. A group of the unattractive, humble children were standing around at the bus stop, not twenty feet from her, playing with portable electronics or staring into space (or whatever it was they did, Lex thought to herself). Just behind them, on the edge of the school property, a group of handsome children were throwing a ball aggressively.

Lex strode past the homely children and through the gate in the chain-link fence separating the school from the street, narrowly avoiding a strapping boy who had been racing to throw a backpack at one of his friends.

As she went, she pulled the hood of her sweatshirt up. Probably this look was more likely to intimidate or impress the kids. Maybe they would mistake her for an older boy or part of a gang. She tried not to overthink it. She didn't want to give herself time to succumb to the fear she still felt, at times, when in the presence of pre-teens and young teens.

"Porn for sale!" Lex cried at last, lifting her sheaf of porn pages. "That's right — I have a stack of genuine adult publications for sale, right here in my hands! Come one, come all, to purchase some of this fantastic porn!"

The kids looked up from their game of sex and aggression.

"What the fuck," said a boy with big horsey teeth and the ugly, long surfer/emo hair that seemingly every suburban eighth-grade boy had that year.

"Pornographic images and stories!" Lex yelled in answer. "Scenes of hard-core fucking! None of this 'making love' bullshit." She addressed the boy with horsey teeth specifically: "You can see girls with enormous tits, who have no shame."

"Gross," said a short, dark-haired girl in a tank top, and made a disgusted face.

"What the fuck, is that actual porn?" said the blond boy who was holding her hand.

"A page is only two dollars," Lex told the kids starting to gather around her. "Think about that! How much did your parents have to give you for that new PlayStation, huh?!"

She waved the sheaf in front of individual kids' faces to show them it was actual porn.

"Ugh."

"Fucking gross!"

"It's actual porn!"

"He doesn't go to this school!"

"I can't tell if its a boy or girl!"

"Give me that!" yelled the first boy, finally, the one with the horsey teeth.

He was another version of Eric from last night. He had the same long-legged, athletic build, except in preteen form. "We can show this to Mr. Berliner," he crowed. He grabbed at the sheaf of porn with a swift, athletic, football-throwing arm.

Lex pulled the porn towards her body in alarm. Just in time – he was strong and fast. He only managed to tear off the top of the first page.

"Don't, uh – don't touch the merchandise," cried Lex. This wasn't what she expected at all.

"I'm serious!" yelled the boy with the horsey teeth. "I'm getting Mr. Berliner!" He started to trot across the field on his long legs, grasping the scrap of senseless pastiche of faces and breasts in his hands.

"You guys tackle him," he yelled when he was halfway across. "Just fucking bring him down!"

The kids closed in on Lex. A few of them kept glancing uncertainly towards where their leader had run off to. Mostly they kept their eyes on Lex, who clutched her sheaf of porn. Lex wondered what was wrong with kids these days.

"Uh, is Mr. Berliner your principal?" she asked.

No one answered.

"Come on," she tried to reason with them. "I remember being your age. I fucking hated authority. I didn't even care what it was, if the adults didn't want me to have it, I wanted it."

"This pervert's gonna get in trouble," the blond boy observed to the girl whose hand he was holding.

Lex began to feel humiliated and angry. This episode – the middle schoolers' simultaneous hostility and lack of interest – was forcing her to recall parts of her past that she would rather have forgotten. And if adults came, she might get in trouble or perhaps be fined. She could not afford a fine.

Lex instinctively ran towards the blond boy's girlfriend, the dark-haired, short girl who had before so easily contorted her face into such a delicate, unselfconscious expression of disgust. This girl was clearly the weakest link in the chain of middle schoolers surrounding Lex. Lex slammed into her with her full body weight. Strategically, this was an effective move. The girl fell swiftly. Lex broke through the crowd of children, and ran away.

Lex ran through the gate in the chain-link fence, past the kids waiting for the bus, across Burnet Road. Cars honked at her, and she kept running. She did not look back. She kept running in the direction she'd come from, towards the house where her unfinished burritos were, where Jennifer was quite possibly having sex again at this very moment.

She didn't get far. Within a few blocks, she came to a stop in the shade on someone's lawn. Between her backpack, her heavy, weather-inappropriate clothing, and her relatively out-of-shape physical condition, she was unable to run farther.

She leaned against a tree, breathing heavily, and prepared for the worst: jail, fines, further humiliation. When no one came, she sat down.

As she rested from her exertions, Lex reflected on how her life had led up to this moment. She thought about failing college. She thought about pornography and emotional pornography, and whether there was any artistic merit in either. She thought maybe she should give *Confessions* another try. It was so hard to concentrate on anything these days. She daydreamed about what it would be like to lie in the shade with a girl she had known in the Speech Language Pathology graduate program at UT. She allowed ants to crawl on her.

5

She was lying on the grass when one of the unfortunate bus-stop kids from the middle school approached her. She knew he was from the middle school because he towered over her and asked, "Excuse me? Are you the porn peddler?"

"What?" said Lex. She scrambled to her feet.

"I believe," said the kid, "I heard you shouting to my peers. You said, quote unquote, that you had genuine adult publications for sale?" The kid made quotation marks with his fingers.

Lex looked at the kid. Puberty had not been kind to him. He had an oily, sort of fat face, unmemorable except for its partial mustache. He himself was neither fat nor thin. There was a picture of a dog in sunglasses on his T-shirt.

"Oh!" said Lex, returned at once to reality. "Um, yes, I do have them."

She had actually been lying on top of her little collection, and now it was scattered on the grass. She bent to gather the individual pages.

"They're, uh, two dollars – one dollar – a page," she said.

"They're only one dollar?" asked the kid incredulously. "Why, I'll take them all!"

Lex was embarrassed at how grateful she felt. She counted out twenty-five pages of bland, stylized nudity and sex. The kid took out a wallet decorated with orange flames, and gave Lex a twenty and a ten.

"Keep the change," he said. He was trying to be jaunty. "You know, I pay top dollar for this stuff."

"Um, thanks," said Lex. "I didn't know."

Lex did her trick of trying to imagine people in eighteenth-century settings. She tried to imagine the kid as a young Rousseau. It was difficult. He looked like some arbitrary kid, strictly of his time. This time she was in.

THE MEANINGFUL EX

Talking to the Meaningful Ex was usually frustrating in a way I could not pin down, but it was different with this visit. This time I actually had something new to discuss. We were going on a walk through the neighborhood at night.

"So he made me eat dog food. Or, rather," I explained, "I made him make me eat the dog food. Newman's Own. Organic brand."

The Meaningful Ex laughed. "I always thought you were a hardy masochist. I'll never forget that time you ate a slug," they said.

"Haha, that could have killed me."

They were talking about high school. They were referring to a time we were all sitting on the grass, me and them and some boys who hung out with us, and I had tried to impress them, the Meaningful Ex, by eating a slug that had been crawling on the grass. This was long before they had "come out as non-binary," so the dynamic between us had been different. The slug-flesh tasted bitter, obviously, and had a disturbing texture, rubbery yet yielding, with a big mass of sticky bubbles that came out when I bit into it, causing the Meaningful Ex and myself to laugh uproariously for some reason. I remember how happy I was to witness the boys witnessing our interaction. It had been a great flowering of life and culture for me – and, I guess, the Meaningful Ex. With them, finally, all those little parts of myself previously confined to my journal – wanting to strike back at an uncaring world, wanting to express my difference with edgy, masculine "jokes" – had an outlet. That was almost fifteen years ago, yet I still think of it as the defining period of my life.

"That slug had the strangest texture, I'll never forget," I said. "Rubbery, yet easy to bite into. Like a hot dog."

"You have such a talent for disgusting me."

"Haha, thanks."

I punched them in the arm. They ran up the street, still in that big black coat they always wore.

"You want to know more," I said. I tried to loom over them physically. In the streetlights, their face looked two-dimensional, just like how I remembered.

"You finally get what I've been trying to tell you."

"What do you mean?" I said.

But I knew what they meant.

I had been telling them about Rex Racer, the whole scene, back in New York, right before I flew back here, after the open mic, with the dog food. The Meaningful Ex believed – they were always talking about this – that in order to be passionate about someone, truly passionate, you had to feel that they were very different from you. Something about them had to be so compelling that it threatened your whole "normal" way of life, with its familiar priorities. It had to force you into a different reality – which meant, for them (as far as I could tell), a state of overwhelming, evil sensuality that made everything else irrelevant, even our precious identities as adolescent thinkers and intellectuals. That was how the Meaningful Ex always described to me, in detail, their relationships with men: a continuous state of desire, a kind of mystical and philosophical "will to evil" which apparently, until now, I was too "good" to understand.

The Meaningful Ex was now saying that they thought Rex Racer caused me to feel that way, the way they felt about the men they dated. They were saying that they thought, from the way I described having sex with him, that the way I felt about him paralleled the way they had felt about Rob and Nate and all the others, back in those days when all that stuff happened and I wrote those long emails (and also maybe how they felt about them now, albeit in a slightly different yet not totally incompatible way).

"No," I said. "I know what you're talking about and this is *not* that."

I thought of the acts I performed with Rex Racer, back in Brooklyn. My whole identity as a man depended on my being able to make the distinction I was now making.

"I *did* feel the thing that you're talking about. The death of the self and all that. But the whole *reason* that it was possible was because I felt that he was *the same* as me. Not 'different.'"

"Huh," they said. "Well, maybe that's true of you."

That wistful note, like they were on the cover of one of those goth CDs.

"Yes. I literally just said that."

"You'd probably never fall in love with someone unless they were intellectually compatible with you."

This felt like it was intended to be an insult.

"You don't get it," I said. "It's not an 'intellectual' compatibility either. Why do you keep trying to *interpret* my experience?"

"You don't want me to help interpret your experience?"

The street was going up into the hills. I looked at the direction we'd come from, the lights below. This was where my parents lived now, in one of the big houses.

"No! Well, maybe! These conversations are so annoying."

That was when we had an argument. I asserted that the Meaningful Ex had used me, relegating me to a sexless "intellectual" role, where my job was to help them process their feelings about the real people, real men, who, for them, were the true sources of romantic passion. They asserted that I was incorrect. They asserted that, in fact, my sexual or psychological need for self-martyrdom – of which the recent dog food-eating incident with Rex Racer was one example, but which had many antecedents during our relationship, including the slug incident, the threesome with Rob, and the time I ate food off the floor at a Chinese restaurant with Demian (it had been regular vegetarian Chinese food, from a plate that we'd put on the floor, rather than from a dog bowl) – they asserted that this need for self-martyrdom caused me to put myself into the position of *seeming* to be used by them; they asserted that, in fact, I actually put them, against their will, into a certain role in relation to me for my own gratification, a maternal, "feminine" role that the Meaningful Ex disliked; they asserted that, in fact, the mere fact that they stayed friends with me, despite my objectionable actions, was evidence of the fact that they, the Meaningful Ex, did not consider me as peripheral as I claimed; and, they said, furthermore, it was ironic of me to say they considered me a "confidant" – when, in fact, I never listened to them talk about *their* life, and that, consequently, most of our conversations, including this current conversation, were about me and my problems.

I admitted to the Meaningful Ex, finally, that their last statement was partially true. It *was* true. I could not participate with them any more in the same way. This discourse used to mean everything, but now it meant less because the Meaningful Ex was not, after all, "the same as me"; their experiences did not mirror mine. It was the price of separating myself from them.

"'From childhood's hour I have not been as others were,'" the Meaningful Ex intoned, sarcastically quoting the Edgar Allan Poe poem/song lyric.

"Shut up!" I exclaimed.

"'I have not SEEN as others saw— '"

This time I actually punched them hard. I twisted their arm, imitating the armlock from the jiu-jitsu class I had taken for a few months last year, as part of the overall project of trying to understand or recalibrate my sexuality.

"Well, maybe its not true!" I said. I struggled to hold on to the wrist of the Meaningful Ex as they kicked my knees and made a dart away from me onto the lawn of one of the massive houses lining the street. "Maybe we are still similar in some ways!"

The motion-sensitive lights in front of the massive house turned on. A dog began to bark. I focused on the image or concept of Rex Racer – a form on the bed of my Brooklyn apartment, a pair of eyes. I wondered what he would think of this interaction.

We ended up walking to the creek behind my parents' house. The Meaningful Ex put their hands in the water and made me feel how cold it was. I was apprehensive about traversing that space, seeing the enormous house my parents had now acquired with its hulking cars, its complex landscaping, its separate lights in my parents' separate rooms, but I went anyway.

We had been walking for a long time, and it was almost morning when I returned to my parents' house. I snuck up the stairs, cringing and furtive. My grandfather's funeral was the next day.

5

I woke up to a message from Rex Racer.

"Maybe we should have a safe word," said the message.

I didn't know how to answer that. It was the feeling I associated with New York, the awkward feeling, after a sex encounter, of being obligated to some person.

"The safe word should be," I typed. I looked through the list of available emojis and picked the red-faced tongue emoji. "When I have this expression."

Did I actually "like" eating dog food? Did I get off on physical pain? I didn't actually know what I liked.

"You may not know this," I continued, "but I am somewhat experienced with pain."

"A safe word would let me be more harsh," smirk emoji.

"Haha, true."

Maybe that is what having a relationship with a person is like. Getting messages and thinking of how to reply to those messages.

"Well, let me think of the proper word," I wrote.

I took a picture of myself against the pastel-yellow-and-white bedsheets in one of my parents' guest bedrooms, the once-awkward contortions familiar after years of being on Grindr and in other adult online spaces.

"I am still thinking," I wrote.

I sent the explicit picture, meant to depict me "thinking." I thought for a long time about whether to follow up with a smile emoji. It was almost eight. My phone rang. I had only been asleep for a few hours.

"Hello! Hello! Wake the fuck up!"

"Hello? What the fuck?"

It was my sister. I often talked to the Meaningful Ex about my family, turning the formless awkwardness of it all into something I could feel pride in and define myself in relation to. I used to speak negatively about my younger sister, portraying her as conventional and feminine. Recently I'd begun to talk about her more positively, with putative admiration. In reality, I had to admit, I was usually too busy thinking about myself and how I came off to really register my younger sibling as a real person.

"Why are you calling me from inside the house?"

"I am helping our mom! The funeral is today. Hello?"

"Yo," I said, playing up my old persona. "Isn't it later in the day?"

No. In fact, the funeral was happening at ten, in just two hours.

I got dressed. In the past, when I lived with my parents, I used to spend hours trying on clothes that I believed de-emphasized my thighs, repeatedly taking off and putting on one of two Old Navy or the Gap men's button-down shirts. That was in the old house, not this large new house they had now acquired, thirty years after emigrating as refugees from the Hanseatic City of Lübeck with nothing but a suitcase and my sibling and myself, but the habit of paralysis remained. I stared at the large futon I had slept on. I recalled the process of moving it to the new house two years ago, arguing with my father about whether or not I was going to help him carry the furniture, and then grimly doing so. When I walked downstairs, my mother was down there, in the large living room, which still, two years later, didn't have any furniture in it. Or rather, any permanent furniture. Currently, a set of folding metal chairs provided seating for guests, and a number of my late grandfather's possessions were piled against one wall. I was surprised to see my cousins from Lübeck seated on the chairs.

"He's here," my mother announced to the assembled family members.

"Hahaha," I said, acknowledging the fact that I had woken up late.

My older cousin (he was my age) stared at my beard. I had grown it out as part of another "inside joke," with Rex Racer and the people at the open mic, about masculinity and body autonomy. It was kind of like the dog food thing, except not part of an official sex scene, but I couldn't explain that here.

"Good morning," said my younger, more sociable cousin.

"Good morning," I said, attempting to imbue my voice with a confidence I didn't feel.

"Your relatives are here," announced my mother to me. "Your blood relatives."

"Yes," I said. "I can see that."

I looked at the big ornate clock leaning propped up against the wall, which I vividly remembered hanging in my grandfather's apartment. I regarded also his collections of Japanese theatrical masks, his stacks of old science books, and his desktop-sized replica of the Venus de Milo, with its wide hips and bland face, its "classical" feminine figure that used to enrage me when I was younger.

"Did you notice they're here?" my mother repeated, as if I had not just stated, semi-sarcastically, that I had.

"Yes, of course," I repeated.

But it was true: I had not been explicitly anticipating their arrival. I glanced apologetically at my cousins. I tried not to make any unnecessary movements. I was about to check my phone when I heard the sound of a sliding glass door opening and closing quickly. My father came in from the backyard.

"Cigarette break?" said my mother, with some hostility.

My father did not answer. He picked up and put down the miniature Venus de Milo statue. He began to speak. There was a specific problem, something had happened.

It seemed that the cemetery had called, saying that the burial service was scheduled for twelve instead of ten, contrary to what everyone (including my sister, who had told me ten) had been led to believe. My father now had to go to the cemetery by himself to redress the scheduling error. This would leave him unable to pick up my grandfather's former caregiver, Mrs. B_____, and drive her to the cemetery by ten, the previously agreed-upon time.

"Well, maybe, um, Origen," said my uncle finally, venturing my legal name, "can drive Mrs. B_____."

Origen was the name I chose after I transitioned to male. In high school (right before I became obsessed with the Meaningful Ex), I played text-based single-player RPGs, and that was the name I would always give to my player characters – Origen – after the third-century theologian. I had never read his works directly, but we had once briefly discussed him in class. I remember the packet said that he had reconciled Christianity with the rational philosophy of classical Greece. Perhaps I had imagined myself accomplishing something similar in the modern day, reconciling the present with an idealized, romanticized past.

"Yes, why not?" said my mother.

"I definitely can do that," I piped in.

But the "why not" was a rhetorical question. I was being blamed for something.

"Look, I can drive whoever it is," I reiterated. I re-checked my phone.

"Hgngng fucking pelvic lines," said the incoming text. It was Rex Racer, finally replying to my photo message.

"Really," I told my parents, emboldened by Rex Racer's reply, "I'm a great driver. And I just saw Speed Racer."

"Can you please stop talking," my sister interrupted in English.

"Fuck off, little sis," I said playfully. "Don't try to tell me what to do."

The family ignored this. My mother continued to look at my father with a displeased expression. My father continued to handle the Venus de Milo statue.

"Does A_____ know how to drive?" my father asked after a while. "Sorry, Origen," he corrected himself.

"Of course I know how to drive."

My parents had bought me a used car in high school, which I used to drive the Meaningful Ex everywhere.

"You let your license expire."

"No I didn't."

We argued about this. My voice rose to an undignified pitch. My father went on to explain the process whereby he had learned about the expired license, via a California DMV notification that had been sent to my parents' address.

"Maybe I have a whole separate driver's license that I got in New York! Did you think about that?"

"You don't trust your own son?" my mother interrupted. "The product, so to speak, of your own loins?"

"Maybe I bought a car in New York," I continued.

My mother implored us to stop arguing. "Listen to what you're saying," she said. She meant that I was arguing frivolously with my father, about the status of my driver's license, while there were far weightier moral and emotional factors in play, related not just to my driving but to the occasion as a whole, everything that was happening and my role in it.

But I thought again of Rex Racer's encouraging answer to my photo message. I needed to assert myself. I played up, again, my status as a liability, indulging in the old teenage mindset. "Maybe I'm simply exempt from these rules due to my role as the Nietszchean 'last man'!" I said.

My father did not respond to the provocation.

〜

Eventually, we stopped arguing. I received a copy of my father's keys. In the car — I was relieved that it was not my father's car, or my mother's, but a third car my parents had bought, gray and nondescript, whose interior provided a partial illusion of anonymity — I immediately messaged Rex Racer.

"I can't think of a safe word, nothing is safe!" I wrote.

There was no answer.

"Sorry, funeral is happening now — it is kind of dramatic," I added.

I wondered if that was a good message. I decided that it was. It was short and contained an apology, as well as a charged, superficially casual glimpse of my life.

I found the upcoming encounter with the caregiver concerning for two reasons. First, we had never actually talked (even though I had once sheepishly waved to her at a family dinner where my grandfather failed to recognise me due to his memory loss). Second, over the course of the two years that she had been his paid caregiver, she had probably formed some unspeakable, good-and-bad, family-type relationship with my grandfather — one that blurred the boundaries between personal and professional — and not just with him, but with my parents and sister, who had probably been asking and paying her to be the emotional and logistical buffer between them and him. And now that he had died, and she was still around, it was unclear what her role was. Would I be blamed for this fraught dynamic?

I pulled up to the house where the caregiver was staying. To my relief, it was located in a "good" part of town, next to the library and "good" public high school, known for its math and science program, which I had attended briefly. I saw her standing outside, wearing sunglasses and the traditional black. She had dark hair and other, normal features, which I was too embarrassed to observe in more detail.

"One second!" I said through the partially open window. I had to check my phone. It was another message from Rex Racer.

"Funerals are hard, I feel that."

I sat without moving for some time, in response to the fresh wave of embarrassment. What had I been expecting, by alluding to what was happening, other than this polite answer? Gesturing apologetically at Mrs. B_____, I composed a message to the Meaningful Ex.

"I just had an awkward conversation with my boyfriend! Need emotional support, urgent!"

They were probably not going to reply, but I needed the sense of having done something. Finally, I opened the door.

"I am so sorry," I told Mrs. B_____, as she quickly entered the car. "My mother keeps sending these urgent messages."

But Mrs. B_____ seemed unconcerned. She got inside and began speaking immediately. To my alarm, she appeared to be visibly upset.

"I'm so sorry," I repeated. "It's just she keeps sending these messages. Well, there was kind of a scheduling error with the funeral, as you probably know."

But Mrs. B_____ didn't seem interested in this either. She kept talking about my grandfather.

"First of all, he was an atheist, so he wouldn't have wanted a 'burial service,'" she started.

"Yes, of course. I guess that's why they said it would be a non-denominational service." I tried to match the serious tone of the conversation.

"He saw the value in religion," she went on. "Protestantism especially. But he didn't practice it."

She continued to talk about my grandfather's social and spiritual beliefs.

"He bought a lot of books," she said.

"Yes," I repeated. "Well, I never got to talk much to him towards the end," I offered finally. "Due to my gender change, so to speak. We were trying not to ruin his memory of me." I could not resist smiling slightly, as if to acknowledge how successful the change was, even by this woman's, no doubt, traditional standards.

"He was open-minded. Eastern Orthodoxy, Catholicism. He respected all of the major religions," she said emphatically.

"Hm," I said.

I wanted her to have a good opinion of me. I was unsure if she was still replying to my comment about the non-denominational service.

"Well, I talked to him a lot in my youth. He was my favorite relative," I told her.

Then I saw part of my face in the rearview mirror.

"I'm sorry about this beard, by the way," I said. "I hope its not off-putting to you. I know it probably looks weird. I'm definitely going to shave it off." I wanted to present myself as an old-fashioned, sensitive man, in spite of, or perhaps because of, being trans – how I imagined she might imagine a younger version of my grandfather. However, I could not tell if my statement had the desired effect, since she did not respond directly to my statements about my facial hair.

Instead, she stopped talking for a while. Then she began to tell me in detail about being in my grandfather's apartment during the last days of his life. She talked about the fear she felt while she was alone with him during this time.

"He was in a lot of pain. It was a terrifying experience," she kept saying.

"To be alone while witnessing that," I said. "I understand."

Maybe that was my role: a neutral, male observer, who could help others put into words the strong emotions I was incapable of feeling myself. The same as what I had claimed to be for the Meaningful Ex. I paid attention to my driving as she spoke, staying under the speed limit, looking straight ahead while switching from Park to Drive in my black clothes.

"It went on for fifteen – no – sixteen hours," said Mrs. B_____, continuing to reminisce.

"My girlfriend is going to meet up with everyone for the service," I told her, after several more articulations.

"What?" she asked finally.

"How do you say it?" I pretended to search for the non-English word. "My girlfriend. She lives here. Even though I live in New York."

"Oh," she said, after a moment. "Well, it's good you have someone."

It was the first time she actually referred to me in the conversation, saying "you," as if acknowledging me, for the first time, as the descendant of the deceased relative. I wondered if I had heard barely perceptible approval in her voice. Maybe, it occurred to me, the dread I felt most of the time, a dread which I was able to evoke at will, made me uniquely capable of comforting this woman.

While stopped at a red light, I texted the Meaningful Ex.

"Please ignore my last message. Could you actually come to the funeral, like soon?"

I knew they had said earlier that they'd try to make it. They had said they needed to go to Oakland that evening – they were conducting one of their weekly Gnostic masses – but that they would try to show up, either at my parents' house or at whatever part of the cemetery the funeral was happening in, in between their preliminary preparations at a friend's apartment (which was close to the cemetery) and their departure for Oakland. Yet I mistrusted the Meaningful Ex's ability to follow the schedules that were such a large part of my family's life. It was actually part of the whole discourse I had with them – the nature of time and timelessness, the ontological status of our future and past selves.

"I hope my girlfriend won't get lost," I told Mrs. B_____.

⌇

When I got to the cemetery, after some thirty minutes of driving and thoughtful, quiet assertions, the Meaningful Ex was not there. I pulled up at the designated space, where I saw my mother speaking at a podium on the grass. I tried to help my grandfather's former caretaker out of the car. She refused.

I looked at the bright-green grass and cloudless, featureless sky, which I remembered thinking of in high school as being uniquely characteristic of my hometown. My mother was speaking to a handful of people: my immediate and extended family, Mr. and Mrs. K____, Mr. and Mrs. M____, and a woman I did not know, who turned out to be the manager at my grandfather's apartment complex. It was possibly out of deference to this woman, the sole person in attendance who was not from Lübeck, that my mother's speech was in English.

"See," I gestured to Mrs. B____. "It's a non-denominational service."

She put on a baseball cap and adjusted it in acknowledgment, as she slowly made her way to the outer edge of the group. My sister embraced her. The baseball cap (the one non-black element of her attire) was branded with the logo of the tech company where my mother had been a manager for the past ten years. I realized that, probably, although my mother spoke English with a strong accent and made many gestures, neither Mrs. B____ nor my cousins would be able to understand her speech.

My mother kept talking. "He actually had a very interesting life," she said. "There were actually many facets to it. For example, he was born in the twentieth century. Maybe you could say he died in the twentieth century – not in the literal sense of course, as it is not the twentieth century now."

She was wearing a black business suit and a woman's fedora-style hat to shield herself from the sun. I realized I had never heard her speak uninterruptedly like this, always returning, uncharacteristically, to the same semi-biographical narrative about my grandfather, rather than stating a series of opinions or moral judgments.

I went up to Mrs. B_____.

"You probably can't understand what she's saying," I told her.

My sister looked at me blankly. I ignored her. I looked at my mother continuing to speak. I felt more sympathetic towards her than usual. I remembered that I, at times, admired her.

"He was very young when he got his first engineering post," she went on.

I started translating.

"Very young. It is possible that he met the Pope? When we opened his papers there were papers in there from the 1940s and '50s. That was at the university in Z_____," my mother elaborated.

I began to imitate my mother's oratorical gestures. It was difficult to simultaneously watch her while positioning myself in such a way as to be adequately in view of my cousins and my grandfather's former caregiver. Yes, the Pope," I said emphatically. "I am trying to remember. Not a modern pope. It was Pius or Innocent, one of those Catholic names. Maybe it was actually the head of the Eastern Orthodox Church?"

Some of the people were watching me and some of them were watching my mother. I heard my voice ring out to the assembled group. It was just as I had always heard it in my head, measured, considerate, with little flourishes of emotion − not overwhelming. Weighing the past and future, musing about the past, contemplating the future. It was the voice from my old journal.

"He was very well-liked at the university. Well, it was probably easier to be liked in those days. He got married to my mother. He always had a woman taking care of him, right up until the end of his life."

My mother paused, seemingly lost in thought.

"She is thinking of what to say next," I explained.

"Can you please stop translating," said my sister.

"Yes, of course."

"Maybe there is something romantic about his life that needs to be preserved. Something that is hard to say what it is. I was not able to relate to him well. When my mother died – his wife— "

I repositioned myself, as if I was about to start talking again.

"Just stop," said my sister.

"Okay. I was just trying to be helpful."

Afterwards, I also decided go up to speak.

"He had that giant grandfather clock in his room," I said. "I was so scared of it when I was young. And now its not ringing anymore."

To my satisfaction, I noticed tears springing from my eyes. I looked at the audience. The Meaningful Ex still was not there. But a little later, when they did show up, in a long-sleeved black dress with a lace collar, jet beads, and fur, wearing some some sort of heavily spiced perfume, it was worth it. I embraced them after I left the podium.

"I told everyone you were my girlfriend," I told them.

⁓5⁓

That night I ended up going with the Meaningful Ex to Oakland. My mother had organized a lunch at my parents' house after the funeral, and, just like the funeral itself (the latter part of it when the Meaningful Ex showed up), it was something of a triumph for me. The Meaningful Ex actually drove back with me, following me and my grandfather's former caregiver, struggling up the hills in their father's car.

Once there, in the living room of my parents' house – one of the few times, I noticed, that there had ever been enough people in the room to fill its vast space – the Meaningful Ex talked to everyone there and did not mention their current boyfriend, whoever he was (perhaps the friend who lived near the cemetery, or their new collaborator in Oakland, whom I had not yet met). They did not do or say anything to contradict the statement that they were my girlfriend, so much that, afterwards, the next day, my mother actually asked me what my relationship to the Meaningful Ex was, and I told her it was none of her business.

Throughout the lunch, adding to my sense of temporary respite, the Meaningful Ex exhibited at most a subdued version of that characteristic naive, slightly barbaric interest in other people, which had always, as I had once put it, fascinated so many of our region's "emotionally impoverished heterosexual men." They asked my sister about graduate school, returned my cousins' inquisitive looks, and laughed in response to non-English statements directed at them by Mr. and Mrs. M____, causing Mr. M____, and, ultimately, even my mother, to laugh at the Meaningful Ex's inability to understand the language. By the time the Meaningful Ex started recounting how they had recently wept at a recital of the Hans Christian Andersen story "The Steadfast Tin Soldier," I felt well enough to slip away into a side room of my parents' house.

It was not the room where I was staying, but another room, unused, piled with old objects from the old house that my mother had been trying to organize (even prior to the recent sudden influx of new old objects from my grandfather's apartment).

I pulled out an old carry-on luggage bag. It had been there last year. It had items from my old room. I quickly found what I was looking for: a black dress that I had worn to my high school graduation, with black ruffled sleeves and fake laces in the front – a primitive approximation of the Meaningful Ex's current gothic style. I looked through my phone to find an old photograph of me wearing the same dress.

"Should I wear this again??" I texted Rex Racer, alongside the old picture of me in the dress.

"Not to the actual funeral, that's over," I added to the message.

"LOL," I added after a while.

I waited a few minutes. It was likely he would reply soon and I would have to think of something to say back. This nervous anticipation invested these interactions with a thrill, like being whipped with a belt.

"Ooh dress and bearded look," said the eventual reply. "I'm jealous."

I looked at myself in the mirrored closet door. Again, I had forgotten about the beard.

"Well, I would shave the beard," I texted.

I looked again at my depersonalized face. "Unless you don't want me to haha."

The joke or idea I had with the beard that I was doing this as a kink for Rex Racer's benefit: making myself assume a false, confusing, avuncular appearance that everyone thought I liked, but I actually disliked. That is, everyone probably assumed I did want to have a beard, since I had gone through all the trouble of transitioning to supposedly make myself look how I wanted, but I did not.

I thought of it as similar to how a stereotypical hetero-sexual woman, in a "bad" relationship, might feel pressured to change her appearance to cater to a man's needs – for example, by undergoing breast augmentation or wearing revealing clothing. By cultivating an unwanted beard, I was pretending to be a woman in a "bad," coercive relationship with Rex Racer, even though I was actually a man, and he was a man, and, therefore, our relationship was not "bad" or coercive, but actually symbolic and important.

I had never said any of this openly to Rex Racer – the symbolism had seemed clear enough. But the combination of the dress and beard made it confusing.

"You should do what YOU want," Rex Racer texted me back.

"Yeah definitely," I answered. "I do love a good beard. Well, in an ironic way, I think," I added.

I looked around the side room, wondering how else I could have replied to Rex Racer's bland responses. Suddenly I didn't want to be there anymore. I decided to return to the living room. I folded the dress on top of the bag.

"Where were you?" asked my mother.

"Don't ask," said my father.

"Maybe a toast?" suggested Mrs. K____, trying to distract my mother. "From your oldest, so to speak, son."

My mother looked at me uncertainly.

"Haha, I don't think so," I said.

"Can I actually go with you to Oakland?" I asked the Meaningful Ex, dreading their imminent departure.

"Seems like your family needs you to be here."

"It's fine."

I assumed that the Meaningful Ex was unsure about me going with them to Oakland because they believed that I was uninterested in their life, and that I would only care about their experiences with Western esoteric mysticism insofar as it pertained to my relationship with them. I assumed they believed that I would conflate their role at the temple with their past and present personal relationships with me and the other people in Oakland. I assured them that it wasn't like that. And it wasn't.

As I understood it, the Meaningful Ex's involvement with the whole scene in Oakland – first the goth clubs, and now the whole temple thing – was a direct consequence of the idea that had been so transformative in our adolescence – the concept that there is a true, psychic world underneath this one, and if you could find a way to reliably access that world, you could have control over what happens in this one too.

Finally the Meaningful Ex said okay. "Maybe it will help you deal with whatever is going on here," they said.

No one seemed to mind. The assertion that the Meaningful Ex was my girlfriend was definitely a success.

The Meaningful Ex's father's ancient car was full of clothes, art supplies, and temple furnishings. I surreptitiously made space for myself in the front seat as we drove.

"Stop touching everything," they said.

"I'm not, I'm only touching some things."

"Remember the time you wiped your snot on my curtains?"

"Haha, I was trying to prove that the phenomena you can't perceive don't exist — but I guess you perceived them."

I expected the Meaningful Ex to laugh at this, and they did, accelerating wildly onto the highway. I turned up the volume in the car's aged CD player (not as old as the car itself), which I had bought for the Meaningful Ex the second time I had moved back into my parents' house, using money from a tech support call center job that I had briefly (this was around the time I ate food from a plate on the Chinese restaurant floor, during one of the antagonistic, email-writing phases of our relationship). We began to listen to Nosferatu and the Machine in the Garden and other goth and darkwave bands from the 2000s and '90s.

But when we got closer to Oakland, the Meaningful Ex became preoccupied.

"Now we're listening to goth music," I texted Rex Racer during the ensuing lull in the conversation.

I looked out at the bay, at the silhouettes of container ships and container cranes. The sun was just starting to set. Rex Racer did not reply, but I had been careful not to anticipate his reply.

"It's definitely romantic, being out here," I told the Meaningful Ex.

"Hm, I'm kind of worried about setting everything up."

We finally got to the house where the temple was, on the edge of an industrial area by the highway. I followed the Meaningful Ex up the rickety porch steps. The living room was filled with the usual black-wearing types, people I used to be so intimidated by in my teens, but who, now, after my experiences of interacting with groups in New York, I no longer feared the same way.

I scanned the group for a likely conversational partner, and was surprised to see Rob there. I realized that this actually made sense. It was natural that the Meaningful Ex and their past boyfriends, who had participated together in the world-changing, metaphysical act of sex, would continue to associate with each other in these other, equally cosmic projects.

"You two know each other," said the Meaningful Ex.

"Hm," I said.

Before I could say anything else, they disappeared behind a curtain.

"Long time no see?" said Rob.

"Haha, yes," I answered.

He looked very different now from how he looked during the time of the ill-fated threesome between me, him, and the Meaningful Ex, but his face still conveyed the same sense of well-meaning, naive wonder. I was surprised by how ashamed I felt. I looked for an escape and saw a trans woman wearing a corset and choker, seated on an oversized pillow on the floor. I quickly walked towards her and introduced myself.

"Hi, I'm Origen."

The woman said whatever her name was, smiling primly. I began the inevitable, innocuous flirtation.

"Nice corset. I'd better sit down."

But suddenly, before I could do so, a third person — a man — extended his hand towards me.

"Origen of Alexandria?" said the man. "Very interesting choice."

"Haha, thanks," I said. "I picked it myself!"

This man wore a black velvet cape and had a hairstyle like a poet of the Romantic period, dark, curly, and shoulder length. He had the conspicuously straight posture of someone who wanted to assert his will over material reality. It was something I recognized in myself, from how I, too, now tried to stand and walk whenever I was in public.

"The church father who castrated himself after an overly literal reading of one of the gospels," said the man, smiling.

"Oh yeah, that's why I picked it."

"Hahaha, I genuinely can't tell if you're being sarcastic."

"Hahaha, I can't either! I guess ambiguity, that's my gift."

I forced a laugh. As part of me already knew without asking, this man turned out to be the Meaningful Ex's primary collaborator at this function — and probably, for all intents and purposes, their boyfriend.

⁊

When it was time to perform the mass, we filed into the adjacent room. The trans woman in the corset and choker led everyone in a recitation of the creed of the Gnostic Catholic Church of the OTO.

"I believe in one secret and ineffable Lord... the Serpent and the Lion... Mystery of Mystery," said the woman.

Just as with the music we were listening to in the car, I could not help but be moved by this language. The semi-darkness of the room, revealing the red-tinged outlines of faces and objects, made me remember all the evenings the Meaningful Ex and I had sat in my high school car. I distinctly remembered myself saying, as we both looked through the windshield at a trash container in the alley behind Happy Donuts, "We can give names to things and describe them to each other, that's what gives us power over them," and the Meaningful Ex had agreed. I have been trying to recreate that moment, that feeling, ever since.

Now I watched them emerge now from behind a curtain. They used a ceremonial sword to pull aside another, second curtain, behind which stood their collaborator, with his shoulder-length hair. He was dressed in a white robe — the priest of the mass. The Meaningful Ex made a sign of the cross over him. The smirk was gone from his face. He looked deadly earnest.

In answer to the Meaningful Ex, he made a series of corresponding, sharp gestures. "I am a man among men," said the priest. He thumped a ceremonial rod on the floor. "How should I be worthy to administer the virtues to the Brethren?"

The Meaningful Ex answered by making the sign of the cross several more times over the man's body. The man put on a red coat. After a while, the Meaningful Ex began to repeatedly stroke the rod that the man was holding. They were clearly emulating a sexual partner — a woman — stroking an enormous phallus. The gesture was both universal yet specific, symbolic yet unpleasantly real.

I thought about what the Meaningful Ex had said about needing the person you are passionate about to be different from you. The Meaningful Ex was different from me. But in some ways they were the same. It actually amounted to the same thing: being passionate about someone, in the way that we had both talked about, meant the dissolution of that pervasive fog, that boundary between you and other people. So it shouldn't matter if they were originally different from or similar to you. And maybe I experienced that with Rex Racer.

"Be the Lord present among us," said the Meaningful Ex, raising their arms above the symbolic rod.

"So mote it be."

As I stood up, I felt my back pocket vibrate. Maybe he was actually texting me back! In the dark, I could not resist the urge to check my phone.

The man, empowered by the Meaningful Ex's earlier ministrations, led the Meaningful Ex across the room to a large altar. The Meaningful Ex sat on the altar. I squinted at my phone, carefully holding it below what I estimated to be the other attendees' line of sight.

Rex Racer had sent me a picture. It was a black-and-white photograph of a man, a fashion photograph. The man had a thin face, a bushy beard, and an elaborately groomed, curling mustache.

The man in the photograph actually looked kind of like me – or, rather, how I used to want to look when I still envisioned myself as a physically frail, intellectual type of man (except for the actual mustache and beard, which I had not fantasized about, but now possessed).

In front of the altar, the priest splashed water and waved incense over the Meaningful Ex. I turned my phone screen brightness all the way down.

"You think I look like that??" I wrote surreptitiously to Rex Racer.

I knelt in a posture of adoration, my hands above my head like in a Pre-Raphaelite painting of a people in a medieval church.

"No I wanna look like that lol," answered the text.

Of course. I continued to kneel, the phone wedged between my knees. A curtain had been drawn in front of the altar, hiding the Meaningful Ex from view. The priest started making a speech in front of the altar. I was sure that the Meaningful Ex was too engrossed in their role as officiant to have noticed me texting.

"Oh circle of Stars... soul of infinite space," intoned the priest.

I attended to the man's loud, theatrical voice. The speech was about the higher-order principle or consciousness – somehow feminine – that was being summoned behind the curtain.

"Let... men speak not of thee as One but as None... and let them speak not of thee at all, since thou art continuous."

Yes, I reflected. Maybe that was why I liked Rex Racer so much. The fact that he wanted to look like what I used to want to look like (except for the beard, of course) now made me feel that same sense of sympathy towards him, and that same sense of vertiginous dissolution of boundaries, that I had felt a few days ago, back in my apartment. And Rex Racer's actual physical appearance – how it shifted constantly when

I tried to visualize it — also made him similar to me. His appearance was not "androgynous" in any conventional way, but also not "feminine" or "masculine." It only made sense with huge quantities of makeup, or a beard, or some other technique to push it into context.

The Meaningful Ex started speaking from behind the curtain. "For one kiss wilt thou then be willing to give all... But whoso gives one particle of dust shall lose all in that hour," they said, in a measured voice.

It was true. When Rex Racer made me eat dog food — when I made him make me eat dog food — in that moment, it changed and redeemed everything. My family, going to soccer practice when I was nine. My past, present, and future humiliations.

"I charge you earnestly to come before me in a single robe, and covered with a rich headdress. I love you! I yearn to you!" said the Meaningful Ex.

On that night, we had posited an alternative reality where humiliation was fake, and where anything could be sex. And positing it made it real. A "performative" act — an expression or statement that performs the act it specifies — like a Gnostic mass, like a ritual. And it was like that with the slug too. After more speeches in the same vein, the man, in a reprisal of the Meaningful Ex's earlier gesture with the sword, finally pulled back the curtain to reveal the Meaningful Ex seated fully nude on the altar. The man fell slowly, exaggeratedly to his knees. I carefully took hold of my phone. It was now the trans woman's turn to speak. I had not seen the Meaningful Ex in a state of physical undress in some time. It did not matter. I finally had the chance to text back Rex Racer.

"Oh I see," I wrote, referencing his earlier photo message of the bearded and mustache-sporting man. "Well, you would DEFINITELY look like that if you started testosterone."

"Lao-tzu... Priapus... Rabelais," said the trans woman. As part of her role in the mass, she was narrating a long list of mythological and historical figures.

"Like a 2000s hipster bartender," I added. There was a time when I would have given anything for someone – for a person with whom I had actually engaged in an important, mutually desired sex act – to be gender affirming like this.

"Merlin... Parzival... Friedrich Nietzsche..."

Wait – maybe he would misinterpret that.

"In a hot way," I amended. "People are always saying they can't tell if I'm being sarcastic haha."

"Paul Gauguin... Doctor Theodor Reuss, and Sir Aleister Crowley..."

I repeated the series of texts in my head. Now it sounded too earnest. "Where is your unicycle lol," I concluded.

Someone nearby coughed. It was Rob. He had been sitting next to me this whole time.

"So mote it be," I said, jamming the phone in my pocket.

Unsurprisingly, Origen of Alexandria was not one of the figures.

☞

After the mass, the Meaningful Ex got mad at me for texting. "The fact that you thought no one would notice makes it slightly more insulting," they observed, fully clothed once more. "But only slightly."

They angrily bit into a piece of pre-sliced white bread, which someone had probably brought to make sandwiches after the mass. We were in one of the bedrooms of the house in Oakland. In contrast to how hot it was in the room where the mass took place, this room was cold, letting in air from the seaport outside.

"Hahaha," I said, shivering slightly. "Well, isn't that one of the rules of Thelema? 'Do what thou wilt shall be the whole of the law.'"

I sipped from a plastic cup of communion wine.

"That," said the Meaningful Ex, "is a stupid statement. You're stupid."

Rob laughed a little at what we were saying. "Stop fighting, you two," he said.

Again, he was seated near me me. His hair was now its natural brown color. He had stopped bleaching it blond. He had gained weight, but still had the same long, thin nose and blue eyes with prominent eyelashes – features that had once reminded me of Philip II of Spain, or a face in an El Greco painting (I had fantasized about this type of imagery in high school, prior to meeting the Meaningful Ex). He also still had the same inquisitive, eager-to-please expression I had found so intolerable earlier.

"This is just how they talk," interrupted the Meaningful Ex's pseudo-Romantic, pseudo-medieval collaborator and likely boyfriend. He was no longer wearing his ceremonial robes. His shoulder length hair hung down over his Renaissance-era doublet, apparently wet with sweat from his earlier exertions.

"They've told me all about it," he said.

The Meaningful Ex, seated next to him on the floor, ignored him for the moment. They wrapped themselves in his cape, which they wore on top of their own faux fur garment (the same one they had worn to the funeral).

"You might have benefited from the presence of the gods. Just saying," they said.

They took another bite of pre-sliced bread.

"And who were you texting? Was it your mom?" they asked sarcastically.

I saw Rob looking at me. "Well, what if it was my mom? We're actually in the middle of a very important and" – I remembered how much I'd dreaded being left alone at my parents' house – "sad family event, so it actually would make sense for my mother to be contacting me— "

"No, you were texting that boy," said the Meaningful Ex. "What's his name – Speed Racer?"

This was so unpleasant to hear that I crushed the plastic cup I was holding.

"His name is Rex Racer!" I shouted.

Now everyone looked at me – the trans woman in the choker (she had unlaced her corset and was lying on a bed in the middle of the room), a couple in matching puffy shirts (they were also lying on the same bed, on either side of the trans woman), and a few other people.

I felt agitated. I slowly picked up the plastic cup remnants and put them in my pants pocket.

At the conclusion of the mass, after the symbolic, mystic marriage between the two opposed polarities represented by its chief officers, I had gone up to the altar with everyone else, and had drunk from the wine goblet and consumed the wafer of light. I had stared up at the nude, seated Meaningful-Ex-as-priestess, and they had responded with a bland, incomprehensible smile, directed, probably, not at me but at some abstract idea of me as a part of broader humanity that had little to do with what I was thinking or feeling. I hadn't gotten any more texts from Rex Racer.

"Don't let them be mean to you," the trans woman interrupted my morose revery.

"Yeah, its okay," Rob put in.

He reached over to pat my leg.

I was startled by the physical contact. The last time I had seen him was two years ago, approximately eight years after the threesome incident. The Meaningful Ex and I had to pick up a folding table at his apartment after their father died, and he had given us a short, apologetic tour, showing us the kitchen, the bedroom, his computer, the display cases for his knives and miniatures. The Meaningful Ex had told me that he was married now, and that it was an open marriage. They had said that he and his wife were maybe even considering having children.

"Um," I said. I turned to the trans woman, facing her in order to dismiss the brief but unexpectedly potent mental image of the Meaningful Ex's ex-boyfriend conceiving a child with his hypothetical wife.

"Yeah no, I'm not letting them be mean to me," I told the trans woman. "I have boundaries."

"Good," she said. She pointed to the bed. "Massage?"

"I would love that."

I clambered onto the bed where she lay between the reclining couple, draping my feet over the male member of the couple's legs. I tried to catch the Meaningful Ex's eye. To my satisfaction, they were still looking at me, frowning, taciturn. Their priest and boyfriend sat next to them, his back to the wall, his posture straight – no longer interested, seemingly, in our exchange.

I submitted to the massage. I felt the woman's fingers linger over my upper body, touching the trapezius muscle I'd been working on these past few years, and the little muscles around the scapula, the teres minor and teres major. The hard structural components of her corset pressed into my back at what I imagined to be her breast level.

Was it true, as the Meaningful Ex had said, that I didn't pay attention to my environment? I pressed my back against the woman's corset and hands. On the contrary, I was constantly aware of my external environment. It was constantly bearing down on me – a barrage of inadequate answers, vague information, ambiguous threats. And I still wanted to transcend that.

"You think queer relationships are inherently boring or something," I asserted. "You need these, like – trappings of conventional heterosexuality to add spice to the relationship, to make it seem 'evil'. It's so dumb."

"I never said that. I never said I wasn't, uh – 'queer'," they quoted.

"You said dating someone who was too similar to you would be boring."

"I said it would be boring to date someone who has the same flaws as me. Who's always asking: 'Am I better or worse than other people?' Always checking their phone— "

"I see," I said.

The Meaningful Ex was quoting (unfairly in my view) from a college application essay I had once written, the second time I applied to college. This particular "essay" had taken the form of a comic strip, in which the last panel consisted of just the sentence "Am I better or worse than other people?" in white against a black background. It was definitely unpleasant to remember that period in my life, showing the Meaningful Ex that essay, asking for their opinion.

I leaned into the woman's massage, as if it were really relieving me of physical tension.

"Well, at least someone – other than me – doesn't think my personality is boring."

The Meaningful Ex closed the package of pre-sliced bread.

"Are you still talking about that kid?"

"Maybe! This really feels good, by the way," I told the trans woman. She kept making the same vague motions around my shoulders and vertebrae.

"You haven't told me anything about him. Like actually about him and not you," said the Meaningful Ex.

"Keep going," I told the trans woman. "I believe I have expressed myself, uh, adequately on the topic," I said to the Meaningful Ex.

"He represents something for you. You're clearly projecting something onto him."

I closed my eyes. The trans woman repetitively stroked my shoulders. I entwined my feet with the lower legs of both members of the surrounding couple, trying not to put my shoes on the mattress.

"I have no idea what I'm doing," said the trans woman.

"You must be intuitively sensitive to my body," I told her.

I opened my eyes. I watched as the Meaningful Ex adjusted their furs and rewrapped themselves in their boyfriend/ collaborator's velvet cape. In a gesture of finality, they threw the bread package at Rob.

"I'm heading out," they said.

"Ow," said Rob.

"You're driving him back," they told Rob, indicating me. "I have to seclude myself in contemplation."

They left the room. Their collaborator left with them, despite their statement about "secluding themselves." Rob, the Meaningful Ex's ex-boyfriend — the second, I recalled, of the meaningful ex-boyfriends, after Nate — looked at me with his permanently concerned expression.

I turned to face the trans woman. "Can you actually give me a ride?" I asked.

She quickly squeezed my lats. "Sure."

⌐

But when the time came for the ride, I knew, as I'd always known, that I was not going to do it. The trans woman was only safe territory up to a point. Going to Oakland with the Meaningful Ex always posed these social challenges. I decided ultimately that the ex-boyfriend actually constituted the lesser threat.

"I changed my mind," I told the trans woman. "He will drive me."

And he did. When I got into his car, he inevitably asked me how I was doing, and I told him a shortened but still overly long version of the story of my life. I mentioned going to the gym, applying for insurance, listening to poetry, taking public transit to sex parties and bars, and heeding calls to help pay acquaintances' rent via crowdfunding and social media platforms.

He, in turn, told me about his life. He was not working at the army surplus store anymore. He expressed surprise that now, after all this time, we both had jobs that allowed us to finance our lives as, in his words, "real adults." We both talked about how annoying it was to have meetings for work, and our preference for the meetings to be remote.

During this interaction, I became provisionally less embarrassed. I imagined that we would continue to talk like this, in this normal, amicable manner, and to fill the time I started making one of my favorite prepared observations, about how the trans scene in Brooklyn was similar to the royal court, not in sixteenth century Spain, but in seventeenth century France.

"Hahaha, I've missed you," he said in response to my statement.

"Cool, thanks," I said.

"I can tell you're much happier now."

These words caused my shame to return. Hearing him tell me how I was feeling – extending his characteristic, well-meaning, misplaced courtesy while, at the same time, referencing our regrettably shared past – made me revert to the old way of relating to others. It was similar to the phenomenon with my parents. I tried to hold on to the persona of the new, "happier" me, but I could already hear the change in my voice.

"Yeah, everything is totally different now," I said.

"You seem more like yourself," said Rob.

"That's a really good way of putting it. I am more like myself."

We were silent for a few moments, listening to 2000s goth music from his car's CD player, which, like the Meaningful Ex, he still had.

"I've changed too," he said after a while. "Obviously." He patted his slightly protruding stomach. "But I mean, uh, specifically in terms of sex and gender stuff I guess."

"Oh? Do you think you might be a trans woman?" I challenged, trying to restore my lost dignity.

"Hahaha, no. Though I did date a trans woman for a while. And before you say anything" – he wagged his finger at me self-deprecatingly – "I know that would make me straight by itself. A straight guy."

"That's cool," I nodded. I did not like how I sounded – agreeing with everything he was saying – but there was nothing I could do.

"I'm not saying it doesn't," he said.

"No. Yes," I agreed.

Rob looked at the road again. He began to sing along to the song "Marilyn, My Bitterness" by the Crüxshadows.

"I hooked up with Alexei last year? The priest at today's mass," he confided after he finished singing.

"Oh wow." I paused. I was actually surprised to hear this information. I could not help trying to visualize the scenario. That man, Alexei, was about the same height as me. I wondered if he was the receptive partner—

"He's kind of pretentious, but I think that helps him do magic. We were trying to summon the dweller-in-the-abyss."

"Uh, did it work?" I said.

"Yeah."

Rob sang along to more verses from "Marilyn, My Bitterness," hitting the steering wheel in time with the synthesized drums. I watched him drive. His short brown hair and puffier face made him look more vulnerable than he had ten years ago. And at the same time, I could see through his shirt that he had also gained muscle as well as fat. I wondered if I should tell him about how finasteride or dutasteride could prevent male pattern baldness.

The threesome ten years ago had happened at my insistence. I had become convinced that the Meaningful Ex's relationship with Rob, their then boyfriend, was, as I had put it at the time, "more than just sexual" and encroaching on "our friendship". Consequently I had asked the Meaningful Ex repeatedly for weeks to arrange the three-person activity. But when the time came to actually perform the act, I had excused myself and just watched.

"That's pretty cool that it worked," I now told Rob. "I mean the summoning."

I checked my phone, as if for guidance. This time, the only message was from my parents, from my father. The non-English letter patterns felt jarring and hostile. I quickly put away the phone. I decided that the only way out was through. This phrase, I thought, seemed like a "Thelemic" enough precept. The idea that I was maybe going to have sex with him now, with the Meaningful Ex's ex-boyfriend, Rob, became more and more prominent in my mind.

"Yeah," he said again. "Well, anyway, I've been going on Grindr a lot more since then."

"Same here hahaha."

"I mean, I dated the Meaningful Ex," he said, using their name. "So you could say I've never been straight."

"That is something we have in common!" I answered.

"My current partner is kind of non-binary."

"I'm dating a guy."

"My partner has a huge breeding kink, so I guess its good that we're having kids!"

"Same," I said.

We both laughed at the same time.

And I actually did have sex with him. He still lived in the same apartment I had visited two years ago, with its miniatures and knife collection. In the bedroom, I saw a computer with multicolored LED lights and a red, furry comforter. He apologized, again, for the mess.

"It doesn't matter," I told him.

The encounter itself was ambiguous and confusing. On the way there, various disconnected images of what it would be like to engage with him — the idea of the "breeding kink" and the various associations around that — had flashed through my mind, and even seemed enticing. Yet the reality of it was distracting. Watching him respond to me sexually interfered with my own fantasy of what I wanted. I could not even believe, in the end, that he really saw me as a woman.

At least, however, the dread I had felt in connection to him was gone. I would not have to talk to him again. I paid for a ride service to get back to my parents' house. Once again, I crept up the stairs, cringing and furtive. On some level, I envied the Meaningful Ex their situation. I wondered if maybe the lack of living family members was what made them able to have meaningful experiences with others. They probably were not as weighed down as me by the past.

⌇

I woke up again to a message from Rex Racer. During the night, he had responded with a heart reaction to my last three messages, the ones about the "hipster bartender," and the unicycle, and the one where I said people couldn't tell if I was being sarcastic.

"Sorry I didn't answer right away," said the message. "I was at work."

"That's fine!" I wrote back. "You don't need to acknowledge my constant anxiety about whether or not people will answer." I added a smiley emoji instead of a period.

"OMG," answered Rex Racer. "You need to be hit with a whip."

I stretched out on the bedsheets. I knew I would soon be feeling the full physical effects of my earlier actions with the ex-boyfriend, the contortions I had facilitated using my hamstrings and core.

"That may be true," I wrote back, adding a wink emoji.

I felt that I was getting better at these conversations. And despite some lingering sense of physical violation, I also felt that I had accomplished something the previous night, as if the words of the Gnostic mass really had somehow helped me clarify my so-called "true will".

"You know me," I wrote. "I am always stressing out about other people's opinions."

I waited a few minutes. I was wide awake yet physically exhausted. This whole past year, I had been waking up earlier and earlier, rarely able to sleep for more than five or six hours.

"Hm can't relate," answered Rex Racer.

"Really?"

I started composing a reply hypothesizing why that might be, the differences and similarities of our life histories and personalities.

"Just kidding. I used to be anxious," came the message. "Well, antidepressants have helped with that."

"That's cool," I answered.

"Yeah. I'm actually pretty laid-back now. I can't be bothered to stress about what other people are stressing about."

Even that was compelling. The idea of "clinical depression," a mysterious yet identifiable darkness. The idea of "someone like me" experiencing that – this coherent thing "depression" – instead of whatever sordid combination of fear and hope I felt at a given moment – compelled me.

"Hm I see. Well, I can relate to that somewhat."

"I call it nihilistic optimism," he texted.

I sat up in bed. It was encouraging to witness this un-prompted outpouring of ideas. It was not exactly like talking to the Meaningful Ex, but maybe it was approaching that type of relationship? I imagined not telling the Meaningful Ex about this conversation.

"But I actually do think there is something valuable about stressing out about other people, to some extent," I wrote to Rex Racer. "Letting yourself be destabilized by them. Allowing yourself to hold that tension, to experience that fear. It is how you know you are really capable of caring and feeling."

I sent the message. It felt as though we were truly communicating. I was waiting to see his reply when my mother walked into the room without knocking. I lay face up in the bed. The sound of the door opening immediately obviated the subtle ideas I had been trying to express via text.

My mother paused in front of the bed, taking in my supine form. I had put away most of my personal belongings, so that they would be unavailable for commentary or judgment, but I had left the orange container of dutasteride pills on the desk. She picked up the container.

"Those are vitamins," I said.

She looked intently at the purposely unlabelled container.

"Okay," she said.

She put the dutasteride container back down. She sat on the bed.

"What did you want to talk to me about?" I asked, pulling the floral bedcover up to my neck.

"Nothing much."

She scrutinized my form on the bed, taking in, I imagined, my masculinized visage, after however many years.

"That woman got on the plane, she flew back to Riga last night," she informed me.

"Good for her?" I said.

"That woman," Mrs. B_____, the one whom I had driven to the funeral, would always think of the Meaningful Ex as my girlfriend. I imagined the idea spreading through the entire Eurasian continent, separate from me, flowing outwards.

"She was a really special person."

"Sure," I said brusquely.

"Where did you spend the night?"

"Here," I said. Then I thought better of it. "No, actually, I was with the Meaningful Ex."

It still felt strange saying their name.

"I asked your father to send you the message asking you where you were, so it wouldn't seem like I was criticizing you. I don't like to text," said my mother.

The conversation went on like this. My mother continually tried to impress something on me, and I pretended not to know what it was. She talked about the importance of family as a concept, the importance of a continuous narrative within our family. She referenced desires, obligations. She mentioned the Meaningful Ex. Did I really think they were part of this family? She implied the answer to be negative, which I took as my opportunity to express hostility. There was nothing to be done.

"They are my real family!" I asserted loudly. (I forgot, in my haste, to use the correct pronouns to refer to the Meaningful Ex, which I attributed to grammatical differences in the language.)

My mother became angry. After we argued, she left the room. I checked my phone again. I saw that Rex Racer had not issued a textual response to my last message, but merely acknowledged it with a heart reaction. I wondered if he would offer more detail later.

I hastily dressed. I was able to overcome the obstacle of clothing-related paralysis by putting on the same pants, dress shirt, and undergarments I had worn the previous day. I went downstairs. My younger sister, cousins, uncle, and parents were there, as before, seated on the folding chairs, as if in an unsubtle twentieth-century play.

"What a fuckup you are," said my sister.

"Sorry," I said.

She did not answer. She resumed talking to my mother about me in a low voice, interspersing her speech with language from pop psychology.

I sat down at one of the folding tables. They had remained standing since yesterday's lunch, filling a portion of the vast room. There were new wine glasses and plates on the tables. I saw that Mr. K____ was gone, but Mrs. K____ was still there. When Mrs. K____ saw me sit down, she suddenly proposed a toast. My father mumbled his disapproval.

"A toast!" repeated Mrs. K____. "Hello," she shouted. "Hello," she called to my mother and sister.

She began to bang a spoon against an empty glass. My mother looked up, displeased.

I quickly stood up. I helped Mrs. K____ distribute leftover champagne into the empty wine glasses. She began to speak.

"I can see that Aleksey Mikhailovich was an important man," she said. "I can see that he was an influential man. Look at all these boxes."

My cousins looked up with surprised interest.

"I can see the indelible effect that he has had on this family."

"Cheers," said my father, in English. But she did not stop talking.

"There is a great significance to his life. Yet you could say, there is also great significance to his death," she continued. "Perhaps his passing represents the passage of the old ways. What I mean to say is — he is the last one, in a certain, perhaps, sense."

She looked around.

"Yes, he is the last one. What I mean is" – she paused again – "everyone in this family who is of the, so to speak, 'old country' has died," she concluded.

My father frowned. My cousins shifted in their seats.

"But now you can live a new life," she finished the speech. She said my mother's name. "Now your beautiful son can live a new life. To a new life," she asserted.

Everyone clapped, uncertainly, except my mother. Everyone drank from the glasses. My mother approached Mrs. K_____. They began to argue. "Where is Mr. K_____ right now?" I heard her ask, saying the woman's husband's name.

My mother and sister entered a quiet discussion with Mrs. K_____. Maybe they were still talking about me, and our fight earlier, or perhaps they were debating the appropriateness of the toast speech. My father went outside. My cousins and uncle continued to sit at the outer edge of the two tables. I checked and did not see a message from Rex Racer.

I looked through the boxes of my grandfather's belongings. I saw a long handwritten document, which I still have not read to this day. It looked like an autobiography, written in English, using simple, grammatically correct sentences. Maybe he had written it while he was a professor at the university in Z_____, or maybe in the United States, when my grandmother was still alive, or maybe when he lived in the Hanseatic City of Lübeck, practicing English. There was also a series of rhyming poems addressed to my feminine name. These I remembered. My mother was probably the same age as I was now, when he wrote those poems.

"Did you know I'm wearing cum-stained underwear right now?" I wrote to Rex Racer.

I pressed Send. Yet as I did so, I was startled to hear a chirping sound issue from my phone. I had accidentally pressed the video call button. My cousins glanced at me. I ran outside. I decided it was too late to hang up the call.

I walked past my father smoking near the disused barbecue grill and pushed my way through a wall of ornamental plants. Their leaves brushed dust into my eyes and nose as I looked up at the phone. I saw his face, Rex Racer's face. He looked normal. I reflected once again that I could not tell what he actually looked like. It was the same way that I often could not tell what my face actually looked like, whether it looked good or bad.

"Oh whoops hi," I said.

"Hi," said Rex Racer.

He appeared to be in his room. He frowned and stuck out his jaw. He was probably adjusting his appearance for the camera.

"Uh, sorry, I accidentally pressed the video call button," I said.

I began to adjust my appearance in the same way.

"Oh, yeah," said Rex Racer, brushing his bleached-orange hair out of his eyes.

"Sorry, its pretty awkward," I said.

I glanced at the stuffed animals on his bed, at the wall with a giant hanging combined rainbow and trans flag, which contained an embedded anarchy symbol.

"Yeah no, I'm sorry. I'm kind of bad at real-time communication," said Rex Racer.

"Yeah no, same."

"Mm," said Rex Racer.

"Okay," I said. I moved the phone away from my face, experimenting with the camera's field of view.

"Well, anyway," said Rex Racer. He frowned and squinted. He looked down.

"See you later?" I asked.

"Yeah," said Rex Racer. "Yeah, I would like that," he repeated.

"Okay."

And I remembered that it had always been like that. Despite his reluctance to engage with me during the call, he actually did seem pleased by the proposition.

I thought of the last time we saw each other, after the open mic, our last so-called "date," which I had recounted to the Meaningful Ex in such meticulous, rapt detail. I recalled how apprehensive he had seemed at the bar, on the train, during the walk to my apartment. And this distance, this apprehensiveness, remained the whole time we were talking about music and books, about the many nuanced ways we were alienated from our environment. It was only at that moment when he pulled himself towards me, and when I decided to allow it, that the boundaries between self and other were dispelled. It was only when we actually committed those acts – those symbolic yet real acts, which contained within them the promise of redemption and which served as a metaphor for life and will. Or maybe it was later, during my memory of those acts. Maybe it was while I pretended to sleep, my arm draped across his beautiful, compelling, amorphous form on the bed, in my tomb-like, rent-stabilized, single-occupancy apartment. But surely, in order for the memory to coalesce, there needed to be something there.

"Um — we can go to the beach!" I said.

"The beach?" repeated Rex Racer.

"Yeah. I just thought of it."

He squinted at the camera.

"Sure," he said after a while.

"Okay," I said. "Well, anyway."

"Yeah," said Rex Racer.

I waved my fingers apologetically.

"Bye!" I said.

"Uh — bye," said Rex Racer.

I looked between the branches of the ornamental plants. I saw my father walking towards me.

"Are you hiding in the bushes?" he asked.

I returned my gaze to the phone camera.

"I really am wearing cum-stained underwear," I said, romantically.

ACKNOWLEDGEMENTS

I want to thank Cat Fitzpatrick, the greatest editor, who made this book possible – working with you was exactly like an inspirational training montage in a movie, but even longer (much longer) and more inspiring.

Additionally, I want to thank Jeanne Thornton for the thousands of hours of moral support and emotional labor she provided while I was writing this book, literally talking through every aspect of it with me (I also couldn't have finished the book without it), and for introducing me to examples of German humor.

Additionally, I want to thank the following people and organizations: Casey Plett and Emily Zhou at LittlePuss Press, Temple Sophia in Oakland, Tenacity Plys, Miracle Jones, Kevin Carter, Caoimhe Harlock, Joseph Sachs, Anika Grangle (the lemon in my eye), Octavia Kohner, Alexis (the boss of Shame Club), Nat Buchbinder, Briana Silberberg, Sasha Karbachinskiy, Raya Terran, Aleksei Postnikov.

ABOUT THE AUTHOR

Anton Solomonik is a writer and illustrator living in Brooklyn. He's the co-host of the World Transsexual Forum, an open mic series for trans writers. His work has been described as, "whimsical, yet heavy-handed." This is his first book.

TYPOGRAPHICAL ΠOTE

Realistic Fiction is set in BC Figural, a digital reconstruction by the Prague-based Briefcase Type Foundry of a "rugged but graceful" expressionist typeface originally designed by Oldřich Menhart in the 1940s. The headings and titles are in a more recent Briefcase font, Marek Čuban's Ludva.